W9-APE-706

Chelsea's Special Touch

#10
Chelsea's Special Touch

Hilda Stahl

CROSSWAY BOOKS • WHEATON, ILLINOIS
A DIVISION OF GOOD NEWS PUBLISHERS

Chelsea's Special Touch

Copyright © 1993 by Word Spinners, Inc.

Published by Crossway Books, a division of
Good News Publishers, 1300 Crescent Street, Wheaton, Illinois 60187.

All rights reserved. No part of this publication may be reproduced,
stored in a retrieval system or transmitted in any form by any
means, electronic, mechanical, photocopy, recording or otherwise,
without the prior permission of the publisher, except as provided by
USA copyright law.

Cover illustration: Paul Casale

Art Direction/Design: Mark Schramm

First printing, 1993

Printed in the United States of America

ISBN 0-89107-712-X

01		00		99		98		97		96								
15	14	13	12	11	10	9	8	7	6	5	4	3	2

*With thanks and love
to my wonderful
Sonya*

Contents

1

The Special Box

Chelsea McCrea sat in the middle of her bedroom floor and spilled out the contents of the packing box. She and her family had moved from Oklahoma to Middle Lake, Michigan, in the spring, and she'd forgotten all about the box. Now that she had a job teaching crafts after school, she needed to look at all the things she'd made. She slipped her favorite puppet onto her hand. "Hello, Sammy."

"It's about time you took me out of that box. I was feeling cramped," the puppet said in a high, squeaky voice.

Chelsea giggled as she dropped the puppet onto the carpet beside her. She picked up a white mouse made of plush fabric, button eyes, waxed thread for whiskers, and a braided cord for a tail. The day she'd made it had been a hot summer day—too hot to step outdoors without wilting. She'd sat in the air-conditioned living room and made the mouse while

Rob sat at his computer in his bedroom and Mike practiced gymnastics in the basement. It had taken her about two hours to finish it. Mom and Dad had thought it was the cutest thing she'd made yet. Her best friend Sidney—at least she was her best friend then—liked it almost as much as the puppet Sammy.

Chelsea chuckled as she looked all around her. She could remember when she'd made each thing.

Just then the other Best Friends—Hannah Shigwam, Kathy Aber, and Roxie Shoulders—walked in. "How cute!" they all cried at once. They dropped to the floor and picked up Chelsea's home-made craft items.

"Where did these come from?" Roxie asked as she rubbed the brown fur of a floppy-eared rabbit.

Chelsea flushed self-consciously. "I made them."

"You did?" Hannah hugged a tiny yellow chicken. "This is sooo cute!"

Kathy touched a turtle made from a walnut shell. "Why didn't you ever show us these before?"

Chelsea shrugged. "I never thought of it. I made them for fun—back in Oklahoma. It's nothing."

"Nothing!" Roxie shook her head. "These are works of art, just like my carvings!"

Chelsea frowned and shook her head. "Nah."

"You have a gift, Chelsea," Hannah said softly. "Not everyone can make things like these."

"Sure they could, if they tried."

The Best Friends shook their heads. They all told why they disagreed, making Chelsea think maybe they were right.

On Monday Chelsea hurried to class and thought about what the Best Friends had said about her "gift." Should she believe them? Laughing and talking students swarmed through the halls. The smell of coffee drifted out from the teachers' lounge. Someone bumped into Chelsea and pushed a folded paper into her hand.

Chelsea closed her hand over the paper and looked around. Who had given it to her? No one was looking at her.

Slowly she opened the paper and read the note:

I WANT TO TALK TO YOU AFTER CLASS. MEET ME IN THE GIRLS' RESTROOM ON THIS FLOOR. DON'T TELL ANYONE—OR ELSE! JOAN GOLNEK

Chelsea shivered. Joan Golnek was about the worst girl in sixth grade, and she wanted to talk to her! What could she want? Chelsea remembered the trouble she'd fallen into when she hung around with the unpredictable Kesha Bronski, before Kesha gave her life to Jesus. But this could be even worse than what had happened then.

Chelsea slowly walked to class. Thinking about Joan Golnek pushed aside all thoughts of her crafts. "I just won't meet with her," Chelsea whispered. "I can't."

The rest of the day she watched out for Joan, and each time she saw her, Joan would slip quickly out of sight. What was this all about? Chelsea wasn't sure she really wanted to know.

■

Tuesday after school Chelsea began to push open the heavy glass door to Malkie's Variety Store, then hesitated. She trembled. Would Joan Golnek be inside? Chelsea's stomach tightened. Joan seemed to keep turning up *everywhere*. Chelsea bit the inside of her lower lip just as Hannah nudged her.

"Hurry up, Chelsea McCrea! It's freezing cold out here!" Shivering, Hannah Shigwam pulled her coat collar up over her neck and chin.

But Chelsea still hesitated. She wanted to say, "Joan might be inside, and I don't want to see her or talk to her," but Hannah wouldn't understand at all, even though they were best friends. Hannah liked Joan Golnek. But then again Hannah liked practically *everyone*.

"Come on, Chelsea!" Hannah jabbed Chelsea between the shoulder blades. "I'm turning into an ice cube right here on the sidewalk." Hannah laughed.

Chelsea forced a chuckle as she pushed open

the heavy glass door and stepped inside. She looked around, her heart hammering. If Joan were inside, Chelsea would leave in a flash and pick up the felt she needed for the craft project later, no matter what Hannah said. Chelsea saw only three other customers in the small store—two small boys near the candy counter and a black woman talking to a sales clerk. Joan wasn't there! Chelsea breathed a sigh of relief. With Hannah close behind her, she passed the cosmetics and the notions and the picture frames and finally reached the counter where the craft supplies were on display.

She wondered again, Why would Joan Golnek suddenly want to talk to her privately? Joan was brash and loud, and everyone said she did drugs. A bright red flush spotted Chelsea's cheeks, making her freckles blend together in one big worried blob. Hannah's chatter drifted over her head and away.

Hannah caught Chelsea's hand. "I thought you said you only needed the blue and red pieces of felt and a few pipe cleaners."

Chelsea looked down at the pile of supplies she'd automatically picked up, and she flushed an even deeper red. "I guess I wasn't paying attention."

Hannah shrugged, then rubbed her hand down her jacket. "You sure weren't! I told you when we were in Penney's that you had something on your mind, and I still say so." Hannah leaned toward

Chelsea and studied her thoughtfully. "Are you afraid of something—or someone?"

Chelsea sagged against the counter, and her blue eyes widened in alarm. "No! . . . Well, maybe." Should she tell Hannah about Joan's note? Chelsea gripped the felt more tightly and wrinkled the corners. Joan had warned her not to say a word to anyone. Shivers ran up and down Chelsea's spine, and she turned away from Hannah.

Suddenly Hannah gripped Chelsea's arm and leaned her head close to Chelsea's. "Oh, look who came in! Chelsea, I'm going to faint!"

"Don't you dare!" Chelsea didn't have to look. She knew the only person Hannah got that excited about was Eli Shoulders, Roxie's brother.

"I wish I was three years older and white—not Ottawa! I wish right now before he gets to the back of the store that I'd turn into the most gorgeous female in all of Middle Lake!"

Chelsea frowned and shook her head. Sometimes she got tired of Hannah going crazy over Eli. "A boy should like you for yourself, not your looks, Hannah."

"Tell that to all the boys who won't even talk to me because I'm Ottawa," Hannah whispered.

Chelsea thumped Hannah and whispered impatiently, "Will you quit it? You said you're glad you're Ottawa because God made you that way—so act like it!"

Hannah sighed. "I will."

Eli opened the heavy front door, the bell tinkled, and he walked out.

Hannah gazed longingly at the door. "He's gone. I wonder if he saw me back here and left so I wouldn't speak to him."

Chelsea rolled her eyes. "Stop it, Hannah! You said you're glad God made you the way you are."

Hannah nodded. "I know. It's just . . .You know."

Chelsea hurried to the checkout counter and paid for the items. Just then she saw her reflection in a mirror, and she frowned at the strained look on her face. Her long red hair looked windblown. The jeans she'd bought with money she'd made from *King's Kids* fit nicely. Some of the bright colors in her jacket clashed with her red hair. She dropped money on the counter, automatically answered the bright comments from the clerk, then finally pushed open the heavy glass door and walked outdoors. Cold wind lashed against her, and she shivered.

"Let's get some hot chocolate before we go to work, Chelsea." Hannah pushed her long black hair out of her face. "I want to jump inside a cup of it just to get warm."

Chelsea glanced at her watch. "We don't have time, Hannah. It'll take a few minutes to get to the church." Chelsea was helping teach crafts at the Middle Lake Christian Center every day after school for the next two weeks. The class was open to children ages five through ten.

"I wish I could've volunteered for something besides being in the nursery." Hannah sighed. "Your job is a lot better than mine! I get bored baby-sitting day after day."

"My job's not always fun. Some of the kids don't want to be in the classes, and it's hard to get them motivated. Usually by the end of each project they're excited, but then it's time to start with a new group."

"I wish I had your talent for crafts."

"You can paint, and I can't do that at all."

"I know. But your crafts look like a lot of fun, especially for kids."

"I guess so."

A few minutes later they reached the church.

Hannah smiled. "I really am glad I could help—even if it is only taking care of the babies of the parents who are helping."

Chelsea smiled. "That sounds more like the Hannah I know and love."

Hannah laughed. "I hate it when I feel sorry for myself."

Chelsea nodded. "I know what you mean. Let's go in."

They ran inside the church and hung up their jackets beside all the other winter coats. Then Hannah hurried to the nursery and Chelsea to the

Sunday school wing. Chelsea had three groups of children who needed to work on the project she'd started yesterday. Laughter floated down the hall. The smell of baking cookies drifted out from the kitchen.

Chelsea stepped inside the classroom that seemed full of ten-year-olds. Most of them were sitting at the three tables. Some of them were walking around the room looking at the pictures on the walls. They were all talking.

Smiling, Mrs. Leeds hurried over to Chelsea. "I'd like you to meet a new girl who'll be with us the rest of the time." Mrs. Leeds lowered her voice. "You'll have to be very patient with her."

Chelsea nodded as she followed Mrs. Leeds to the first table.

Mrs. Leeds rested her hand on a girl's shoulder. "Chelsea, this is Robin Lockwood. Robin, Chelsea is your craft instructor."

"Hi, Robin." Chelsea smiled, but the girl just stared at her, then looked down at her folded hands. Robin was dressed in a pink sweatshirt that clashed with her hair and freckles. Giggling, Chelsea touched her hair and rubbed her arm. "We have something in common."

Robin scowled but didn't say anything.

"Call me if you need help, Chelsea." Mrs. Leeds tugged her blue and white sweater over her blue slacks, then walked toward another group of children who were shouting and laughing as one boy tossed a wadded paper into the air and caught it again and again.

Chelsea opened her pack and lifted out small bags. She called off each name that she'd printed on them. As the boys and girls pulled out the items in their bags, she printed ROBIN on a bag and handed it to her. "We're making puppets from felt and scraps of material."

Robin held the bag without opening it.

Chelsea started to say something to Robin, but the sad look in her eyes stopped her. She instructed the others on what to do, and when she finally had a spare minute she sat beside Robin. "Here, Robin. Take the felt and scraps out. It's fun to make a puppet."

Robin kept her hands folded in her lap and didn't seem interested in anything that Chelsea showed her. Voices buzzed around them.

"I'm ahead of everyone, so I can help Robin," Melody Boyer said as she flipped back her long blonde hair.

"Thanks, Melody." Chelsea slowly walked around the table, then stopped behind a boy named Ralph. "I see you need a little help, Ralph." His puppet looked like a ragged, limp piece of cloth with colored spots. He'd used too much glue, and the colored scraps were soaking wet.

Chelsea glanced across the table just as Melody

reached for Robin's blue felt. Her eyes blazing, Robin grabbed it and held it against her thin chest.

"That's mine, and you can't touch it! I'll make it if I want. You do yours and leave me alone!"

"Well, excuse *me*," Melody said sarcastically as she slid away from Robin. "See if I offer to help again."

Chelsea hurried around to Robin. "I'm sure you can do it alone." Chelsea smiled at Melody. "Thanks for offering your help. I appreciate it."

"I want a needle with blue thread," Robin said sharply. She hooked her tangled red hair over her ears and waited.

Chelsea fumbled around in her bag and finally found the pack of needles and the blue thread. She handed them silently to Robin, then watched as Robin easily threaded the needle and began to sew cut-out circles on the blue puppet's face instead of gluing them as the others had done. Before long Robin's puppet had large white circles with smaller blue ones for eyes, a pink nose, and a wide red mouth. It was a very colorful puppet and by far the best one done.

"I like it," Chelsea said with a pleased smile. "You have a lot of creative talent, Robin. Will you show the others what you've done and tell them why you sewed the things on instead of gluing them?" She knew that it looked better and stayed on better, but she wanted Robin to tell the others herself.

Without speaking, Robin held the puppet close to her and looked down at the cloth-strewn table.

A whistle shrilled, and Chelsea stood at the head of the table with the large box open. "It's time to put your puppets in their bags and hand them in to pack away for tomorrow."

"I want to finish mine." Robin's mouth was set with determination. "I don't want to do nothing else!"

"It's time to work on basket weaving," Chelsea said firmly but kindly. "Tomorrow you'll be able to work on your puppet again." She took the bags from the others, and they ran across the room to another table.

"I am going to stay right here!" Robin lifted her chin and looked angrily at Chelsea, daring her to object. "You can't make me move!"

Chelsea looked helplessly toward John Alexander where he sat with the others, waiting to supervise the basket weaving. Mrs. Leeds was busy with another group, so Chelsea turned back to Robin. "Please put away the puppet and go to the other table. You'll enjoy making the puppet more if you don't work too long at a time on it."

Robin frowned in thought, her eyes narrowed, then slowly pushed her things into the bag and held it out to Chelsea. "I like you."

Chelsea's brows shot up in surprise. "Why, thank you."

"I like you because you know a puppet's face shouldn't be glued on." Robin walked away with her head high and her back straight.

Chelsea thoughtfully watched Robin. *Heavenly Father, show me how I can help her*, she prayed silently.

Much later Chelsea walked tiredly to the front door of the church to wait for Hannah. When she saw Joan Golnek skid to a stop on her bike in front of the church, Chelsea stiffened, then looked around wildly for a place to hide.

Joan pushed open the church door and walked in. She was dressed in faded jeans and a bright orange jacket. Her brown hair was combed back off her wide forehead. She narrowed her blue eyes. "I want to talk to you, McCrea." Joan always called everybody by their last name.

Chelsea glanced around, but she was the only one in the hall. "How'd you know I was here?"

"Your mom told me when I called."

Shivers ran up and down Chelsea's spine. She tried to speak but couldn't. Did Joan know she was nervous? She forced a polite smile. "Why did you want to see me?"

Joan shrugged. "I just did."

"I'm waiting for Hannah." Chelsea's voice cracked, and she frowned down at the floor.

"You afraid of me, McCrea?"

Chelsea lifted her head. "Should I be?"

Joan grinned. "No way! You're smart, and I figure I need a smart friend."

"I'm not that smart."

"I saw all them photographs you took. You got a ribbon for one of 'em."

Chelsea waited. Where was Hannah when she needed her?

Joan pointed at Chelsea. "I want you to teach me how to take good pictures."

Chelsea frowned. "Join the Photography Club and you'll learn."

"I don't have the money."

Chelsea licked her suddenly dry lips. The least she could do was answer politely. "I'm sorry, but I can't teach you."

"Yeah? I say you will."

Chelsea shivered at the look in Joan's eyes. "I don't have time."

"Then make time!"

Trembling, Chelsea stepped back. "But how?"

"Nobody says you have to teach craft classes. Right?" Joan narrowed her eyes. "You could quit these so you can teach me."

"But I can't just quit." Chelsea's voice broke. Why couldn't she just tell Joan to leave her alone?

Just then Hannah walked up. "Hi, Joan. Hi, Chel."

Chelsea was never so glad to see anyone in all her life.

"Hi, Shigwam." Joan lifted her hand. "I gotta be going." She pushed open the door, letting in a gust of icy wind, then pedaled down the sidewalk and away from the church.

Chelsea sighed in relief. "She's really really strange."

"She's all right. She's from a bad neighborhood. Her mom deserted them, and her dad has to work hard to pay the bills."

Chelsea frowned. "How do you know?"

"My dad told me."

"We better get home before it gets dark out." Chelsea didn't want to think about Joan.

At The Ravines, the subdivision where they lived, Chelsea said good-bye to Hannah and ran over to her house. Ezra Menski's dog Gracie ran through her yard, and she frowned. Dad didn't like having Gracie around, and Mom said she always dug holes in the lawn. Chelsea fumbled with the door handle and finally opened the door.

Rob jumped around the door and shouted, "Boo!"

Chelsea jumped and almost dropped the bag she was carrying. "Cut it out, Rob." He was thirteen years old and loved computers.

"I just wanted to welcome you home. Mom and Mike are still gone. Mom said Mike might have to practice gymnastics a half hour later tonight, and you and I are supposed to start dinner."

Chelsea rolled her eyes. "What are we having?"

"How about pizza?"

"Sure. I'll make the salad." Chelsea hung her coat in the hall closet and set the bag on the steps to take up later.

In the kitchen she washed her hands and slowly dried them. "Rob, do you know Joan Golnek?"

Rob turned from the cupboard. "I've seen her around school. Her brother Hank is in my home-room. Why?"

"She wants me to teach her photography."

"Will you?"

Chelsea frowned. "No! Why should I?" She trembled. Would Joan make her sorry for her decision?

2

Robin

Chelsea's stomach cramped with hunger as she looked at the chef's salad Dad had made for supper. For two days she'd hardly eaten, but today she was really hungry. Everything was going to be all right. Joan hadn't stopped her in the hall at school or come by the church. Maybe she'd given up the idea of learning photography. It had probably been a crazy impulse.

Chelsea took the salad bowl Rob held out to her. "Looks great, Dad." Chelsea smiled, a smile that wasn't forced for the first time in two days.

Glenn McCrea nodded, and his eyes twinkled. "Thanks, Chelsea. I'm glad you're going to eat, not just pick at your food again. I was beginning to wonder if you were on a hunger strike."

"It wasn't a hunger strike. I just didn't feel much like eating." Chelsea filled her plate and handed the salad to her mother.

"I wish I had that problem. My new job makes me want to eat all the time. I'm wondering if I should quit." Billie McCrea poured ranch dressing onto her salad. "What do you think, Glenn?"

"You're used to doing secretarial work, not writing a column for the newspaper. You're probably nervous. Give it a few weeks and see."

Chelsea listened to her family talk while she slowly crunched a carrot and enjoyed the salad and a ham sandwich. She smiled at Dad. He was vice president of Benson Electronics and loved his job. When she was younger she'd thought he had the most important job in the whole world, just as important as being President of the United States.

"The Murphys got a new dog," Dad said with his fork in midair. "It's a big black mutt, and it must hate joggers. It actually attacked me when I ran past their house." Dad chuckled. "Maybe it's a sign I should quit trying to get in shape."

"No way!" Mom shook her finger at Dad. "You promised!"

"Dog or not?"

"Yes!"

Dad laughed. "I guess I'm stuck."

Chelsea liked the way laugh lines spread from the corners of Dad's twinkling eyes to his graying hair.

"I'd hate to have a dog attack me," Mike said. "If I had one, I'd train it never to attack."

Chelsea grinned. Mike was always trying to get Mom and Dad to let him have a dog. But they didn't think it was fair for a dog to be tied up or kept in a small pen, so they always told him no.

Rob leaned forward. "You should get yourself a can of mace, Dad. You know, the stuff you spray in a dog's face when he tries to bite or attack."

Chelsea frowned. Rob had once been afraid of everything and everybody, but now he wasn't. He probably wouldn't even be afraid of Joan Golnek.

Dad laughed and said, "I bought a can of it before I came home this afternoon. That dog is in for a surprise tomorrow if he attacks me."

"You be careful, Glenn." Mom reached over and squeezed his arm. "I don't want you coming home with only one arm. I'm partial to that arm."

His eyes wide with shock, Mike dropped his napkin onto his empty plate. "Dad, I think you should take a pocketful of dog biscuits and make friends with the dog. That would be better than hurting him with the spray."

Smiling, Dad nodded. "You're right, son. I'll do just that! And I'll tell the dog he has you to thank."

Mike swelled with pride.

Just then the phone rang, and Chelsea jumped, then flushed as the others looked at her and laughed.

"It isn't alive, Chelsea," Mom said as she hurried to answer it. "It just seems like it at times."

Chelsea dabbed her open mouth with a paper

napkin, then dropped it beside her flowered plate. Often the Best Friends called, but never at a meal. Would Joan call? Chelsea's stomach knotted, and she looked down quickly to hide the sudden fear in her eyes.

What would she say if Joan did call? How would she act?

Mom turned from the phone. "It's for you, Chelsea."

"For Chelsea?" Rob scowled, and his shoulders drooped. "I thought it might be Nick. We're working on a computer game together."

The color drained from Chelsea's face as she slowly walked across the room to the phone. She reached for it, then dropped her hand to her side. "I'll take it in the study."

Mom nodded, a watchful expression on her face.

In the study Chelsea took a deep breath and lifted the receiver. Perspiration popped out on her forehead as she said hello.

"Chelsea, this is Peter . . . Peter Stone."

She sank down on the high-backed plush desk chair. "Peter?" Why on earth would he be calling her? He was an eighth grader, and she barely knew him.

"I've been thinking about you lately. You're always an inspiration to me in photography class. What are you working on now?"

Chelsea twisted the cord and thought of the tall, blond boy who had sat beside her in the club. Why would he bother calling her? She cleared her throat. "Mostly I've been teaching crafts."

"I heard you're great at creating things, Chelsea."

Her brows shot up in surprise. "Who from?"

"Alyce Leeds is my aunt."

"I didn't know that."

"She told me all about you and your work."

"I enjoy it," Chelsea said uneasily. What on earth did he want? He'd never called her before.

"Will you have a table at the Arts and Crafts Show?"

"Me?" Her eyes widened. "Why would I?"

"You have all the talent you need, and I know you have projects already finished that you could sell. You could easily set up a table and sell your work."

She moved restlessly. "I hadn't thought about it," she said hesitantly. She wouldn't tell him that she could never find the courage to do it. She'd created her things for her own pleasure—not to sell.

"Sign up to sell your crafts, Chelsea! You're good!"

She frowned in agitation as he talked on and on about the art show. Why in the world had he called her about the show? This was very strange.

After a while Peter was silent.

Chelsea bit her bottom lip and frantically searched her mind for something to say. She clutched the phone more tightly, and her palm grew damp with perspiration. Why didn't he hang up?

"Chelsea, I really called to see . . . if you'd go to a movie with me Friday night."

Her red brows shot up to the hair stretching across her forehead. What was going on?

"Chelsea? Will you go with me?"

She shook her head, and her heart raced in panic. She couldn't say, "I'm not allowed." Instead she blurted out, "I have plans Friday night." The Best Friends were having a sleepover at her house, so she'd told the truth.

"Maybe another time," he said stiffly,

For a fleeting moment she felt sorry for him and almost told him the rest of the truth. Barely above a whisper she said good-bye and dropped the receiver in place with a clatter. Why had he asked her out? He'd never bothered with her before, except for a casual conversation about photography.

She leaned back, gripped the arms of the chair, and rubbed her foot on the soft carpet. She looked at the bright colors of the study. The room was usually relaxing, but she felt coiled tight like a spring that was about to break.

What was happening to her life?

The phone rang, and she jumped and squealed a tiny squeal, then slowly, reluctantly answered it. It couldn't be for her again, but it was, and she sat forward with the receiver gripped in her hand.

"This is Gwen Osborn, Chelsea. I'm Robin Lockwood's foster mother. Robin has told us all about you and your crafts. She is very impressed with you, and so far you're the only person she responds to."

Chelsea cleared her throat. "I know Robin enjoys creating things, and so do I."

"Today Robin sprained her ankle, and she can't be on her feet for several days. She is very distressed, to say the least, because she has to miss art with you. Would you please come talk to us and see if we could arrange for you to come to Robin every day and work with her?"

Chelsea rubbed her free hand across her leg and thought about the sad little girl. "Sure, I'll come see you. When do you want me?"

"How about right now?"

Chelsea hesitated. One of the rules of the *King's Kids* was to always check out the person before accepting a job. She'd better do it this time too, even though it wasn't a *King's Kids* job.

Chelsea cleared her throat. "I'll ask my parents and call you right back. Give me your address and phone number, please." Chelsea wrote it all down, then hung up. If she did go, what if Joan was waiting outside for her? Cold sweat popped out on her forehead, and she closed her eyes tightly.

In the kitchen she told her family about the call. "Do you know the Osborns?"

"We don't, but I'll give Beryl Shigwam a call." Mom hurried to the phone, talked a while, then turned to Chelsea. "She says they're a fine family. It'll be okay for you to go. It's only a couple of blocks outside The Ravines. Be sure to be home before dark though."

"I will."

"I could ride with you," Rob said.

Chelsea smiled. "That's okay." She and Rob were friends, unlike most brothers and sisters she knew. She phoned the Osborns, then grabbed her coat and hurried to the garage for her bike. The wind was down and the temperature up, so it was pleasant weather for a ride.

"Hi, McCrea."

Her eyes widened as Joan Golnek wheeled her bike into sight. She wore jeans and a bright red jacket with blue pockets.

"Where are you goin'? I'll ride with you."

The color drained from Chelsea's face. "I have business."

Joan shrugged. "So?"

"I'm going to the Osborns'."

"I know where they live."

"I'd rather go alone."

"Too bad!"

Chelsea shivered, suddenly panic-stricken at

the thought of Joan riding with her. She glanced out of the corner of her eye at Joan and saw the determined look on her face. Chelsea moistened her dry lips with the tip of her tongue. "Why are you so set on going with me?"

"To talk." Joan frowned. "Shouldn't we get going?"

Chelsea hesitated, then pedaled onto the street, past the houses that looked like twins dressing differently to keep from looking alike, and out of The Ravines.

"I tried to call you last night, but your line was busy," Joan said a little too loudly.

Chelsea's stomach knotted, but she didn't answer. A few minutes later she stopped outside a two-story white frame house with a wide front porch with a swing on it.

"This is it," Joan said as if she'd led the way there. "We'll talk later."

"Don't wait for me. I don't know how long I'll be."

Joan shrugged. "I ain't in a hurry."

Chelsea laid her bike against the porch and ran up the steps. Her hand shook as she knocked on the front door. It was opened immediately by a woman dressed in jeans and a light blue sweater. She had shoulder-length light brown hair and wide hazel eyes. The smell of popcorn and the blare of the TV drifted out around her.

"Hi. I'm Chelsea McCrea." She was afraid to look over her shoulder in case Joan was still there.

"I'm Gwen Osborn, Robin's foster mother. I'm so glad you came!" Gwen held the door wide. "Come in!"

Chelsea stepped into the warmth of the living room. A flowered couch sat against one wall where a man sat reading. A TV rested against another wall, and two kids lay on the floor watching it. A piano with music books open on it stood across the room. Chelsea slipped off her jacket, and Gwen Osborn took it and hung it in the closet.

"My husband Mel and I took Robin in, but now we're having a little communication problem with her." Gwen ushered Chelsea into the living room. "Chelsea, this is my husband Mel and our children Jeanna and Bob."

"Hello," Chelsea said, feeling shy.

"Hi," Jeanna and Bob said, then turned right back to the TV.

Mel smiled but didn't get up. "Thanks for coming, Chelsea. Let me know if you need me."

Gwen pushed her hair back with a trembling hand. "Mel just carried Robin to her room. She was very upset. I sincerely hope you can help her."

"I'll try." Chelsea bit her lip. What could she do?

Gwen led her to the hallway away from the blare of the TV. "Could you come each day after

34

you're finished at the church? We'll pay you, of course." She named a price that surprised Chelsea since she'd already agreed in her own mind to do it for nothing.

"I'll come if Robin really wants me to."

"She will!" Gwen looked as if a heavy weight had been lifted off her, and she smiled. "Let's go tell Robin." Gwen led the way upstairs and knocked on the bedroom door, then walked in with Chelsea behind her. The soft green walls went well with the yellow and white of the bedspread and curtains.

Robin was sobbing into her pillow.

Gwen touched Robin's shaking shoulder. "Chelsea's here." Gwen smiled at Chelsea. "I'll leave you two alone."

Chelsea nodded. She watched Gwen walk out and click the door shut.

"Can we talk, Robin?" Chelsea sank to the edge of the bed and touched the girl.

She lifted her orange-red head and stopped sobbing. "What are you doing here?"

"Mrs. Osborn called me and told me about your ankle. She knew you didn't want to miss craft classes, so I came to talk to you about it."

Robin pushed herself to a sitting position, crossed her thin arms, and stuck out her pointed chin. "I'm going to the church tomorrow no matter what!"

"There's no need." Chelsea smiled. "I'll come

here to work with you—I'll come every day until you can go to the church again." Chelsea saw hope spring up in Robin's eyes. "We'll work together, and we'll have fun."

A slow smile spread across Robin's freckled face. "I'm glad you came, Chelsea."

"Me too." Chelsea took Robin's hand. "I want you to know that I love you, and God loves you even more."

Robin wrinkled her nose. "Gwen and Mel talk about God to me, but I didn't think you would."

Chelsea smiled. "Why not? God is my Heavenly Father. I talk about Him a lot."

"You talk about crafts a lot too."

"I know. God made me creative, and He made you that way too. We like to make things with our hands." Chelsea tapped Robin's freckled hand. "I'm going to show you how to make a mouse paper holder out of a mouse trap, bright material, and half a styrofoam ball."

"You are? When I lived at home I made all kinds of things." A great sadness filled her hazel eyes. "I hate it here! Those little Osborn kids are such babies, and not just because they're younger than me. They don't know anything about crafts. They don't even know how to make a puppet out of a paper bag!"

"I know what you mean. I have an older brother who'd rather sit in front of his computer all day and a younger brother who lives for his gymnastics. He wants to be in the Olympics someday." Chelsea grinned. "They don't care a thing about making things. They couldn't make a puppet or a mouse paper holder or even a simple flower if they tried, which they wouldn't. But God created them the way they are and us the way we are. God created the Osborn children the way they are too, and they are as important to Him as you are."

"Well . . . I guess so."

"You and I are going to have fun making things together."

With a satisfied sigh Robin dropped back down on her pillow. "I'm going to sleep now so tomorrow will come quicker."

"I'll see you before dinner tomorrow, and I'll bring the things we'll need." Chelsea stopped at the door and looked back at Robin in the twin-size bed. "Sleep well, Robin." A great yearning to help the little girl swelled inside Chelsea, and tears stung her eyes. Silently she prayed for Robin as she walked back down to the living room.

Gwen motioned to her. "Please, come sit down a while so we can talk."

Chelsea sank to the edge of the sofa and locked her hands around one knee. Was Joan getting so tired of waiting that she'd leave? Chelsea sure hoped so!

Gwen brushed tears from her eyes. "Robin is at

ease with you, Chelsea. I'm glad! We want to help her and we love her, but she won't open up to us. We know from the caseworker that Robin was badly beaten and that her mother deserted her. But Robin won't say who beat her, and she won't talk about her mother. If she ever talks to you and tells you what happened to her, please listen to her and do what you can to help her. Maybe you can show her that she can trust us."

"I'll do what I can." Again Chelsea thought, *What can I do?*

"Thank you. I know you're a Christian, and I know God will help you know what to do for Robin."

Chelsea slowly stood, and Gwen stood too. "I do have to leave now, but I'll see you tomorrow."

"Thank you for coming! You'll never know how much we appreciate it."

A few minutes later Chelsea stepped outdoors, and a refreshingly cool breeze blew against her flushed face. Soon it would be dark. A dog barked, and someone turned a TV up loud. Reluctantly she walked to her bike.

Joan stepped from around a tree. "You sure took your time. I was beginning to think you'd spend the night."

"You didn't have to wait, you know. I came to talk to Robin."

Joan caught Chelsea's arm and held it firmly. "You're gonna help me too! Right?"

Chelsea bit back a gasp of alarm.

"I don't know why I bother with you, Chelsea McCrea!"

"I don't either! I told you I was too busy."

Joan's eyes filled with tears, and she quickly brushed them away. "I told you I need your help! Can't you understand at all?"

Chelsea helplessly shook her head.

Joan jumped on her bike and rode away at breakneck speed.

Chelsea pedaled toward home. She remembered the tears in Joan's eyes, and compassion began to surface in her. Should she help Joan after all? But if she did, what danger would she be putting herself in? No matter how hard she tried, she couldn't escape the terrible thought.

3

Arts and Crafts Information

Chelsea hurried into Penney's with Hannah to buy a blouse Hannah had seen on sale. With Hannah chattering happily about going roller skating, Chelsea was able to keep her mind off Joan. For most of the week Joan had been on her mind—and even in her dreams. Impatiently she pushed thoughts of Joan away and forced herself to concentrate on the window display of Christmas gifts.

Hannah lifted the shiny blue blouse off the hanger. "I'll try it on and be right back."

"Okay." Chelsea waited near the fitting rooms. A leaflet on the Arts and Crafts Show caught her attention. She bit her lip, hesitated, then picked it up and read it quickly. Would she have enough courage to enter her crafts? Would anyone buy her things if she did? She frowned and dropped the leaflet on the pile as several customers walked around the women's wear department laughing and talking.

Smiling pleasantly, a well-dressed clerk asked, "May I help you?"

Chelsea shook her head. "I'm waiting for a friend."

Hannah poked her head out of the fitting room, her dark eyes sparkling. "I finally found a blouse that makes me look good. I'll be out in a minute. I think I'll buy a dozen of them." She laughed and disappeared.

Chelsea slowly walked toward the heavy glass front doors, her purse in her hand. She was dressed in jeans and a white knit sweater with a scoop neck. A butterfly necklace rested against her throat. Her hair was brushed away from her face and curled down her slender back.

Just then the door opened, and Peter Stone walked in. He smiled happily at Chelsea. "I thought it was you, Chelsea. I was across the street at the drugstore and saw you." His blond curls were bleached from the sun, and his blue eyes looked bright against his sun-tanned face. He was tall and lean. A lot of girls fell for him.

She forced a smile. "Hi, Peter."

"What's new with you, Chelsea?"

She had to look up at him to meet his eyes to see if she could tell what he really wanted to know.

Was he looking at her a little too intently? "I'm still teaching crafts to kids. How about you, Peter?"

He grinned and tugged at his jacket collar. "I'm doing what I do best—a lot of nothing." He narrowed his eyes. "Did you think any more about the Arts and Crafts Show?"

"I saw the brochure on it, and I'm thinking about it." She moved restlessly. Why didn't he leave?

"I hear you're teaching the Osborns' foster daughter."

"How in the world did you hear that?"

"I live three houses away from them, and my mother talks to Gwen Osborn all the time. My mother thinks it's wonderful for you to do that for the little girl."

Something in his voice made her realize that he didn't agree with his mother. "I enjoy working with Robin. She has a few problems, but she's coping, I think."

Peter looped his thumbs in his front pockets and stood with his feet apart. He tilted his head and narrowed his eyes. "Chelsea, you should spend your extra time getting ready for the Arts and Crafts Show. How can you go if you don't have a table full of crafts?"

She cleared her throat and twisted the strap of her purse. A tall man walked around them, pushed open the front door, and walked out of the store, letting in a blast of cool air. Chelsea moved restlessly.

"I'm not going to have a table at the show." Why was she bothering to tell him?

His brows shot up. "You're not? Why? I can't believe that you wouldn't want to. I thought I'd convinced you to do it!"

She narrowed her eyes suspiciously. "Why are you so concerned, Peter? What is it to you?"

He flushed.

She stepped closer to him, close enough to smell peppermint on his breath. Something was wrong, but she couldn't put her finger on it. "Why, Peter?"

He shrugged and forced a laugh. "I'm only thinking of you, Chelsea. If I had your talent, I'd do something with it. Here I am stuck playing football and any other sports my dad can think of. I don't have the talent or the time to be a photojournalist like I planned."

She wagged her finger at him. "Not so! I do remember that you have talent."

He held up his hands and grinned sheepishly. "I must admit that I don't want to work as hard at it as it would take to be successful. Maybe if I wasn't in sports . . ."

"So don't do sports."

"Tell my dad that."

"Oh, come on! He must be proud of your photography."

"Drop it! I was talking about you. You really should get a table. It's only five dollars, and you'd make that back in no time." He made it sound easy and promising and even exciting. "I just happen to have an application for you to fill out. I know Monday is the deadline."

Reluctantly she took the paper. "You really are keeping up with it, aren't you? Are you sure you aren't entering because you don't have the courage?" Had she really said that? Would he realize that that was why *she* hadn't entered the show?

Just then Hannah rushed up, stopping short when she saw Peter. She looked from Peter to Chelsea and back again, and a knowing smile crossed her face. Chelsea wanted to strangle her. "I'll see you later, Chel. Call me when you have time."

"I'm going with you, Hannah," Chelsea said sharply.

"No." Peter caught her arm as he shook his blond head. "You and I are going to get a pizza."

"See you, Chelsea." Hannah pushed out the door with a jolly laugh.

Chelsea frowned at Peter and ran after Hannah. "Wait, will you?"

Several people walking along the sidewalk stopped chattering and laughing and stared at Chelsea. A car honked in the intersection.

Chelsea stuffed the paper into her purse as she caught up with Hannah. They were late, so they ran all the way to the church. Chelsea was glad she didn't have time to explain Peter to Hannah.

Later Chelsea knocked on the Osborns' door. She felt rushed and breathless.

Smiling, Mrs. Osborn opened the door. "Robin thought you weren't coming, but I assured her you would."

"I'd call if I couldn't come."

"That's what I told her. She insisted someone called to say you weren't coming, but I think she was dreaming." Mrs. Osborn pushed the sleeves of her red sweater up. "She's in the family room."

"Thanks. I'll get right in there." Chelsea hurried to the family room where Robin sat at a large table with crafts scattered around her.

"Chelsea! You did come!"

"Of course. It looks like you've been busy."

"This is my favorite," Robin said as she held up a papier-maché ladybug on a broad green leaf cut from plywood and covered with cloth. It smelled like glue. "I think I did a good job, don't you?"

Chelsea nodded. "I'm very proud of you. You do beautiful work. Better than most adults even."

Robin beamed with pride, and a smile spread across her freckled face. "At home I did lots of things." The smile faded, and she looked down at her trembling hands.

Chelsea laid her hand over Robin's. "I know something happened at your home that upset you a

45

lot. Anytime you want to talk about it, I'll listen and help in any way I can."

Robin shook her head and jerked her hand away.

Chelsea sat quietly a while, then picked up the back of a ladybug and sewed a red dot on it. Silently she prayed for Robin. Somehow she had to help the troubled girl. Suddenly she thought about the paper in her purse, and she laughed with delight. "Robin, how would you like to be in the Arts and Crafts Show? You could have a table with me—we could display our crafts together, and people would buy the things we've made." Had she actually said that?

Robin's eyes grew large and round. "I would love it! I've gone to art festivals before, and I've always wanted to be in one. And now I'm going to!" She threw her arms around Chelsea and hugged her hard around the neck, then pulled back, her face red. "I better finish my ladybug."

Chelsea laughed softly. "We both better. We have a lot to do before we're ready for the Arts and Crafts Show."

Later, after getting permission from the Osborns for Robin to be in the festival, Chelsea filled out the form with Robin hovering over her making suggestions and comments. Chelsea pulled a five dollar bill from her purse, and Robin found an envelope. Chelsea read the name and address where she was to send the entry fee, and her heart stopped, then raced on, almost strangling her. Treva Joerger's mother was the person taking the applications and the fee money! Treva was one of the meanest kids in their whole middle school! If Treva learned about Chelsea's being in the show, she would probably laugh and make fun. She was good at that—very good.

Chelsea's hand shook, and she dropped the ballpoint pen. She could not enter! She wouldn't have Treva persuading the entire middle school to laugh at her frail attempt to compete in the show.

"Robin, I've changed my mind. I don't want to be in the Arts and Crafts Show, but I'll fill it out for you and help you." Chelsea's voice trailed away at the wild look on Robin's face.

Robin doubled her fists and scowled with anger. "Who cares about the show? I was only going to do it to help you out. I hate crafts! I hate this ladybug!" She grabbed it and tugged on it and pulled it off the leaf, leaving an ugly tear in the green material.

Chelsea caught Robin's hands and held them tightly, even when Robin tugged to be set free. "Listen to me, Robin. Listen!"

Finally Robin grew quiet, but she kept her head down and wouldn't look at Chelsea.

"I was upset about something for a minute, and that made me lose my courage, but I was wrong. We are both going to put our crafts in the show, and we're going to be as brave as we can be, and we're going to succeed!"

Robin sniffed hard. "Are you sure?"

"I'm sure. I'm not always brave. I get scared, and I let my fear keep me from doing what I want to do, but I won't this time. We are going to go to the show, and we're going to have fun!"

Robin studied Chelsea, then finally smiled. Noise from the TV in the living room made a soft background sound. "I can make a new ladybug, and it'll be better than this one." She held up the tattered bug. "I think it's really terrible that anyone would rip apart and hurt something so pretty." She lifted wide hazel eyes to Chelsea. "Some things that are ruined can never be fixed, can they?"

"What things, Robin?"

"Things." Robin ducked her head.

Chelsea waited, then said, "God can mend broken hearts, Robin." Chelsea heard her own words, and she smiled. Every word was true!

Smells of pizza drifted from the kitchen, and Chelsea looked at her watch. "Hey, it's time for me to leave. I'll see you tomorrow. We'll make arrangements to work on projects for the show."

"Thanks, Chelsea." Robin looked as if she were going to say more, but she turned away and mumbled good-bye.

Chelsea gathered up her things and made her exit. She shoved the envelope into her purse so that when she got home she could stamp it and send it on its way. Her stomach fluttered, but she forced the scary feeling away. It was settled—she and Robin were going to be in the art show!

At the end of the sidewalk she stopped dead and stared in dismay. Joan sat waiting on her bike, a scowl on her face.

"I'm in a big hurry," Chelsea said in a small voice. Her collar suddenly felt too tight, and a muscle jumped in her cheek.

"I only want to talk to you. You could take time to get to know me, you know."

Chelsea cleared her throat. "I could, I guess." What could it hurt? "I have to get home before dark though. Don't you?"

Joan shrugged.

At home Chelsea put her bike in the garage and faced Joan. "I always help make dinner, so I can't stay out here and talk to you right now."

"I'll leave you alone as soon as you say you'll help me."

"I told you I can't!"

"And I said you're going to." Joan narrowed her eyes. "Or else."

"All right—I'll try. But I won't promise!" What had she done?

Joan laughed and pedaled away.

Chelsea rushed to her room and leaned weakly against the closed door. Why had she agreed to try to help Joan? Maybe she could agree, then not do it. She could keep putting Joan off until she got tired of waiting for her. She shivered. Why didn't she feel good about her plan? She knew what she'd decided wasn't right. And besides, she couldn't keep talking to Joan. What would the others in school think of her? What would the Best Friends say?

After dinner Chelsea finished loading the dishwasher as the phone rang. Mom answered.

"It's Hannah, Chelsea. She wants to know if you're ready to go skating. Her dad's taking you."

Chelsea hesitated. Would Joan show up? Chelsea frowned. She couldn't let that stop her plans with the Best Friends. "Tell her I'll be right over."

"See you later," Dad said, giving Chelsea a quick hug.

Chelsea smiled and ran outdoors, slipping her jacket on as she ran.

Hannah waved and called, "Hi. We're going to have fun tonight!"

Chelsea mumbled hello and sat in the backseat with Roxie and Kathy.

Giggling, Hannah looked over her shoulder. "I hope I can stay on my feet all night. I hate when I fall."

"It's been a while since I skated," Chelsea said.

"Me too," Roxie said.

Kathy pushed back her blonde curls. "I go

sometimes with my brothers. They're both a lot better than I am."

At the rink the parking lot was crowded, and Chief Shigwam dropped them at the front door. "I'll be back in two hours. You girls be out here waiting."

"We will, Dad," Hannah said as they all thanked him for the ride.

Several boys and girls stood near the door, laughing and talking loudly. Music blared out from inside.

"Here comes a gang of little kids," Hannah said with a sigh. "Maybe we should've come another night."

"It's too late now," Kathy said.

Roxie held the door open for the Best Friends.

"Chelsea, Chelsea!" Melody Boyer cried, grabbing Chelsea's arm. "I didn't know you were coming tonight! Will you skate with me? Come meet my friend that I brought." Melody tugged Chelsea away. Two boys pushed between her and Hannah. Smells of smoke, body odors, and popcorn made Chelsea's stomach churn. She followed Melody to a short, brown-haired girl. "Carla, this is Chelsea," Melody said proudly. "Chelsea's the girl who helps us with crafts at the church. This is my best friend Carla Reeds. She's going to go to crafts with me tomorrow."

Chelsea talked to them, then helped them put

on their skates. She held her skates at her side as she stood on the sidelines and watched the girls skate away.

Just then Joan skated up and stopped beside Chelsea. "You're good with kids."

Chelsea forced back a frown. Couldn't she ever get away from Joan? "I like kids," she said stiffly.

A small boy fell almost at their feet, and Joan quickly lifted him up, dusted him off, and sent him on his way again.

Chelsea stared in surprise. "You're good with kids too," she said.

Joan shrugged. "I like 'em."

The hum of skates almost drowned out the music as Chelsea tied her skates. She stepped out onto the rink.

A new song started, and Joan yelled, "I like this song. Don't you?"

Chelsea nodded.

Just ahead the same young boy fell, and once again Joan picked him up and dusted him off.

A warmth spread through Chelsea, and she smiled at Joan. Maybe she wasn't as bad as everyone said.

Skaters kept swooshing past them. Hannah skated past and smiled at Chelsea, then glanced at Joan and back to Chelsea. Chelsea flushed and ducked her head.

Just then Joan nudged Chelsea and pointed across the rink to Treva Joerger. "You've got trouble."

Chelsea frowned. Treva was tall and beautiful and was wearing a red silk blouse and tight jeans. Her red lips were parted in a pout. Chelsea bit her bottom lip to force back a sharp remark. "What are you talking about?"

"Treva's out to get you. She's mad because you're good in photography and crafts."

"That's crazy. She barely knows me."

Joan shrugged again. "I heard my brother talking about her."

Chelsea skated to a bench and sank down on it. Joan skated on past.

Just then Melody and Carla dropped down beside Chelsea, one on each side.

"Are you tired already, Chelsea?" Melody asked as she flipped back her long hair.

"A little," Chelsea said.

"How come you're talking to that girl Joan Golnek?" Carla asked.

Chelsea flushed. "Why shouldn't I?"

"She's a bad girl," Carla whispered.

Chelsea gasped. Even the little girls had heard about Joan!

The girls were quiet as Melody retied her skates. "After we're done with the puppets, what'll we make, Chelsea?"

"Something that doesn't take as much time."

Chelsea glanced at Joan as she stopped to talk to Treva. They looked Chelsea's way. The hairs on the back of her neck stood on end. Why would Joan warn her about Treva, then talk to her as if they were sharing secrets? Abruptly Chelsea pushed thoughts of Joan and Treva aside to answer Melody. "I think maybe we'll make turtles out of walnut shells. That'll be fun."

"I might quit going," Melody said gravely.

Chelsea looked at Melody in surprise. "But why?"

"Me and Carla can't be around girls who hang out with Joan Golnek. Our moms said so."

"But I don't hang out with Joan! She happened to be here, and she stopped to talk to me."

Melody shrugged. "Okay. We'll tell our moms." They excused themselves and skated away.

Chelsea sighed and folded her hands in her lap. Slowly she turned her head and looked again at Joan and Treva, still deep in conversation. Chelsea's stomach knotted. Just what was going on?

The music and other noises blared in her ears and pounded against her head, and she shrank into herself. A hand touched her shoulder, and she jumped, then looked up to find Peter Stone smiling down at her.

"Are you alone?" He dropped down beside her.

She shook her head. "I came with friends," she said stiffly.

He grinned and bobbed his eyebrows. "Joan Golnek? I saw you two skating together."

Chelsea locked her icy hands together. "I came with those girls skating over there."

Peter watched the Best Friends for a minute, then turned back to Chelsea. "Did you fill out the form for a table at the Arts and Crafts Show?"

Chelsea nodded.

Peter laughed. "Good." He pushed himself up. "Gotta go." He skated away and right over to Treva Joerger.

Treva Joerger. The name stuck in Chelsea's throat. First Joan, then Peter. Chelsea shivered. What was going on?

4

The Sleepover

Chelsea took a deep breath and let it out slowly. She looked around the circle at the Best Friends. They were sitting in her rec room, knee to knee. All of them were tired after roller skating, but were too excited to go to sleep. She couldn't begin to sleep after what had happened. No matter how hard she tried to find an answer to Peter Stone, Treva Joerger, and Joan Golnek, she couldn't. There *was* no answer! Dare she tell the Best Friends so they could help her? What would Joan do to all of them if she did tell?

Yawning, Roxie pulled her sleeping bag around her shoulders. Her cap of dark hair crackled with static electricity. She looked over her shoulder at the small kitchen and the microwave oven. "I should've brought a bag of chips so we could make nachos."

Kathy groaned. "How can you be hungry? We had hot chocolate, peanut butter cookies, and an entire plate of vegetables and dip." Kathy sniffed. "I still smell the hot chocolate."

Roxie grinned. "I like nachos best."

Hannah studied Chelsea thoughtfully. "Well, are you going to tell us or not?"

Chelsea flushed, her skin becoming as red as her hair. "What do you mean?"

Smiling, Hannah wagged her finger at Chelsea. "Do I look dumb to you? I'm not! We all know something's been bothering you."

Her dark eyes wide, Roxie leaned forward. "What is it?"

Kathy tapped Chelsea's knee. "As best friends we pledged to tell our troubles to each other so we could talk about them and pray for each other."

Chelsea sighed heavily. "I know." She picked up a throw pillow and hugged it close to her. "I don't *know* what's happening. That's why it's bothering me so much."

Hannah's eyes widened. "Is it a mystery?" She loved mysteries!

Roxie shivered. "I hope it's not scary."

"Or boring." Kathy giggled. "Just kidding!"

Chelsea took a deep breath and told the Best Friends about Joan and Peter and Treva and Robin and about the Arts and Crafts Show. "I'm sure there's no connection. But why did Joan talk to Treva after Joan said Treva was making trouble for me? And why is Peter so determined to get me into the Arts and Crafts Show? And how can I discover what—or who—Robin is so afraid of?"

Laughing, Hannah clapped her hands. "This is sooooo wonderful! It's like a whole batch of mysteries all rolled together. I'll put my deductive reasoning to work and see what I can unravel."

The others rolled their eyes and shook their heads.

"I say let's pray first," Roxie said. "I know how much trouble we get in if we forget to pray first." They were all surprised that Roxie was the first to think of that. She really was learning to live like Jesus!

Everyone nodded. They all remembered different times when they had neglected to pray. Problems always seemed gigantic when they didn't ask God for help.

"Here's a Scripture . . ." Hannah looked around the circle. "'If anyone lacks wisdom, ask God and He'll give to it to you.'" Hannah giggled. "It's not a direct quote, but it's close."

Kathy lifted her hand just as if she were in school. "I'll pray."

They all held hands and bowed their heads while Kathy prayed for wisdom and help. She ended with, "Thank You, Heavenly Father, for always being with us and helping us. We'll listen to You and do what You say. In Jesus' name, Amen."

Chelsea dabbed tears from her eyes. Why had

she waited so long before praying about her problems? This was great! She wasn't alone! God was with her to help her. And so were the Best Friends. She smiled around the circle. "Thanks," she whispered hoarsely.

Hannah hugged Chelsea. "Friends should always pray together."

"And play together," Kathy said, giggling. Then she sobered. "I know Joan Golnek causes trouble in every class she's in."

Hannah flung her arms wide. "I just had a brilliant idea! Let's *all* spend time with Joan. Let's *all* do something for her."

"Great idea!"

Roxie nodded. "And we'll stay with Chelsea as she teaches Joan photography." Roxie turned to Chelsea. "That way you won't ever have to be alone with her."

Tears welled up in Chelsea's eyes. "Thanks," she whispered around the lump in her throat.

They sat quietly for a long time. Finally Kathy cleared her throat. "Ty Wilton actually talked to me again today."

Hannah frowned. "Did you tell him to get lost?"

"I tried." Kathy lifted her hands helplessly. "He won't believe me when I say I'm not interested in him any longer."

"Have Roy Marks tell him," Roxie said

sharply. She'd given up her love for Roy because he and Kathy liked each other and had since kindergarten.

Chelsea nodded. "Good idea."

"He said he would." Kathy sighed heavily. "But I hate for Roy to do it because Ty will get really mad and maybe punch Roy in the nose."

"That would be terrible for Roy!" Roxie shook her head. "He doesn't like to fight." Roxie held out her hand. "I'm not saying he's a coward. It's just that he's really nice and doesn't like to hurt anyone."

Kathy frowned at Roxie. "I know."

Roxie bit her lip and stopped talking.

Hannah clasped her hands over her heart. "Eli's really nice too." She turned to Roxie. Eli was her brother. "Does he have a girlfriend yet?"

Roxie shook her head. "He's shy around girls. But Dad says he'll get over it when he's a little older."

"I hope he waits for me." Hannah flushed and looked embarrassed. "But I guess it won't happen that way. He's sixteen, and I'm only twelve and a half."

They talked a little longer about boys, and then Chelsea changed the subject to the Arts and Crafts Show. "Roxie, will you have a table?"

"No—but only because I don't have enough carvings. Mom thought about being in it herself, but she only enters juried shows." The girls looked as if they didn't understand. "That means Mom must send colored slides of several of her carvings. Then a jury judges them. If they think Mom's work is good enough, they let her in."

"Don't they do that for this show?" Hannah asked.

Roxie shook her head. "It's nice to have a show that doesn't, so anyone can enter."

"Anyone like me." Chelsea thought about the entry form and fee she'd mailed today. "I just hope nobody laughs at my crafts."

The Best Friends scowled at Chelsea. "Why should they?" they all asked at once.

Chelsea giggled. "Okay, okay! I guess I'm feeling really unsure of myself."

"God is with you always," Hannah said softly.

Chelsea smiled and nodded. She was thankful she had best friends to remind her. Suddenly she yawned. "I gotta get to sleep. I have to go to the park with Mike in the morning. Mom said it was going to be warm enough for it."

The next morning Chelsea yawned, then yawned again as she slowly followed Mike to the park. He was so excited about meeting three of his friends to practice gymnastics that he wouldn't wait for Chelsea.

At the park she walked slowly across the grass to a green bench. Maybe she'd fall asleep while she waited for Mike to finish practicing. Thankfully the sun was warm. She leaned back and closed her eyes. Two boys from her craft class called to her. She sat up and waved, then yawned.

Just then she heard someone behind her, and she turned with a smile, expecting to see another student. The smile froze on her face. Peter Stone and Treva Joerger stepped to the side of the bench. Why were they here? Had they come to see her?

"Hello," she said hesitantly, looking from one to the other, waiting for something but not knowing what. The air tingled with tension.

"How are you, Chelsea?" Peter asked with an uneasy smile.

"Just fine," she said stiffly.

"Is Joan here?" Treva stood with one slender hand on her narrow waist where a white knit sweater met black pleated pants.

Chelsea frowned. "I have no idea. Why?"

Peter and Treva exchanged quick glances that sent shivers down Chelsea's spine. Something was up, but what? Why would they think Joan was here?

Treva turned her big brown eyes on Chelsea. Sunlight flashed on her blonde hair, making it look like a halo around her head. "I understand you're taking your tacky little homemade things to the Arts and Crafts Show. Doesn't it embarrass you to do that?"

The sudden attack surprised Chelsea. Her

tongue stuck to the roof of her mouth, and her heart raced. The shouts and laughter in the park buzzed inside her head.

"You'll do anything to attract attention, won't you?" Treva stepped so close, Chelsea could smell her perfume. "It won't work. Everybody will laugh."

Pain shot through Chelsea. She pulled into herself, her head down, her eyes closed tightly.

Peter touched her shoulder. "Are you all right?"

"Don't feel sorry for her, Peter," Treva snapped. "She's all right."

Tears stung Chelsea's eyes, and she blinked hard. She would not cry in front of them!

Peter twisted his watchband and looked uncomfortable.

Treva tugged on Peter's arm. "Come on."

Peter pulled free, cleared his throat, and moved from one foot to the other. "Chelsea, I'm sorry if I hurt you. I want to help you. I only pushed the art show on you as a joke."

Chelsea's eyes widened. "What?"

"Cancel your table and get out before you get hurt even more."

Chelsea jumped to her feet. "I don't believe you!"

"I thought I could do anything for Treva, but I can't hurt you."

"Stop it, Peter!" Treva slapped his arm. "I'm leaving, and you'd better come with me!"

Chelsea lifted her chin and looked at Peter. Deep inside she felt God's strength rising until she was engulfed in it. "I don't know why you're saying any of this, Peter, but it's too late to back out of the show. And I wouldn't if I could. Robin and I are in it together."

"You'll be laughed right out of it," Peter said with a red face. "Treva will see to that."

Treva jabbed Peter's arm. "You're impossible! Chelsea can take care of herself. She doesn't need you." Treva tugged on his arm, but he pulled free.

"Leave me alone," Peter said sharply.

"Well, excuse *me*!" Treva ran lightly across the grass to the sidewalk.

"Chelsea . . . please . . ." Peter looked pleadingly at Chelsea. "I'm sorry for tricking you and for hurting you."

Chelsea clenched her hands at her sides. "Just leave me alone."

"You're a nice girl. I'd like to be friends, but I'm sure you'll never forgive me for what I've done." Peter pushed his fingers through his blond hair. "Treva always manages to get me into trouble."

"You're big and strong, Peter. Why be her puppet?"

He shrugged, then grinned sheepishly. "Good point, Chelsea. I'll let you know if I do anything about Treva. We've been helping each other get in and out of things for so long that I guess it's hard to quit." Peter tapped the end of Chelsea's nose with a long finger. "I'll see you. And if I can, I'll help you get out of the Arts and Crafts Show."

Chelsea shook her head hard. "No! I'm staying in!"

"Chelsea . . . Chelsea . . . You'll be embarrassed and laughed right out."

"I'll take my chances," she said stiffly.

He sighed, then turned and walked quickly away.

Chelsea sank to the bench again, shivering uncontrollably. So Treva thought her crafts were tacky, did she? And Peter had convinced her to enter her crafts just to give Treva something to laugh at. Chelsea's stomach cramped painfully, and she moaned. What had she gotten herself into?

Several of her students walked toward her, and she turned away from them and ran blindly toward the restroom. She couldn't face anyone. In the restroom she closed the heavy door, shutting out the shouts and laughter. The strong smell of disinfectant stung her nose. With a sob she splashed cold water on her burning face, then dabbed it dry with a rough paper towel. She doubled her fists and scowled, then caught a glimpse of her reflection in the faded mirror and laughed shakily. Big, bad Chelsea. She couldn't scare a flea off a dog. "Tacky little homemade things, huh!" Her eyes flashed, and the terrible words rang around her head until that was all she heard. Would the people who came to the show think her things were tacky little homemade things and laugh at her? Would she leave the show without selling one item? She pressed her hands to her hot cheeks. How could she get out of going?

From deep inside her she heard the gentle words, "I'm always with you to help you."

She lifted her head high and squared her shoulders. "That's right! Thank You, Jesus."

Chelsea faced herself in the mirror. "I refuse to allow Treva's ugly words to stop me from entering the show!" A slow smile crossed Chelsea's face. She thought of the hours and hours of work she'd done with her crafts. Most of her things were originals. Dad had said he'd help her make a bright display case, and both Mom and Dad had been very impressed and supportive when she'd told them her plans.

"Good for you, Chelsea," Dad had said, hugging her tightly.

"You can do anything you set your mind to doing. You have talent, and you have courage," Mom had said.

Now Chelsea nodded, and her reflection nodded back. "You are right, Dad. Mom, I do have courage! And talent! I am going to succeed!"

Chelsea sniffed and dabbed tears from her eyes. Two girls walked in, and Chelsea slipped out the door into the bright sunlight.

5

Joan Again

Chelsea walked slowly to the park bench and sat down. She watched Mike and his friends doing flips and handstands. Thoughts of Treva's visit and her harsh words took her mind off Mike. She frowned. She had to put Treva and her ugly words totally out of her thoughts!

"Hello, McCrea."

She turned with a little shriek to find Joan Golnek standing there. She looked tired and pale. "How'd you find me?" Chelsea asked.

"Your dad told me." Slowly Joan walked around the bench and sat down. "If you have time, could we talk?"

Chelsea gnawed the inside of her bottom lip. "I guess."

Joan looked closely at Chelsea. "Are you mad at me?"

"I just don't like to be used."

She frowned. "Used? What do you mean?"

"Treva Joerger! I saw you talking to her about me."

"So?"

"So, are you helping her hurt me?"

Joan shook her head hard. "No! I told her to stop talking about you behind your back."

Chelsea narrowed her eyes. Was Joan telling the truth? "Why would you do that?"

"Because you said you'd help me. I was trying to do something nice for you."

"Really?"

Joan nodded. She looked as if she were telling the truth.

Chelsea locked her fingers together in her lap and fought against the burning tears that stung her eyes. Was it possible she'd only expected the worst from Joan because of her bad reputation? Was her reputation only partly true? "Can I believe you?"

"You can trust me, McCrea. We got us a deal, and I won't do nothing to break it."

"Do you know I have a table at the Arts and Crafts Show next week?" Chelsea studied Joan intently.

She nodded. "Treva told me. She sure did laugh. I almost punched her in the nose."

"I'm glad you didn't."

Joan took a deep breath. "Do you really think your stuff is good enough? Your things will be right next to artists from all over Western Michigan. Can you handle that?"

Chelsea blanched. Even Joan wondered! "Whether I can or not, Joan, I'm going to do it. Robin and I have a table together. She's been working hard getting crafts ready to sell."

"If you think you're good enough, then so do I."

"Really?"

"I'd sure like to see what you have."

"So you can laugh at it? No thanks! If you want to see my crafts, then come to the show and take a good long look. You might even find something you'd want to buy."

"Hey, I might!"

Chelsea flushed. She had tried to be sarcastic, but Joan had taken it as a real invitation. "Treva thinks my things are tacky homemade things."

"So who cares what *she* thinks?" Joan laughed. "Did you see her photographs? She takes worse pictures than me. But she's not about to let somebody else help her." Joan jabbed Chelsea's arm. "But I am! You're gonna help me, and I'll get awards and everything!"

Chelsea smiled. Suddenly she *wanted* to help Joan. "I sure am going to help you!" She would too—with the Best Friends right beside her to keep her safe.

"When can we start?"

"After the Arts and Crafts Show. Then I'll have time."

Joan sighed. "I don't know if I can wait that long, McCrea."

"Call me Chelsea."

Joan swallowed hard. "I don't know if I can."

"Try it. It's easy. Just say *chel sea*." Chelsea giggled.

Joan jumped up. "You making fun of me?"

"No. I'm trying to be friends. Honest."

Joan brushed at her eyes. "I gotta go." She dashed away, her hair bouncing on her back.

Chelsea frowned thoughtfully. Was Joan afraid to become friends? Was Joan afraid of *anything*?

Later Chelsea walked Mike home, then pedaled to the Osborns to work with Robin. Mrs. Osborn answered the door, a haggard look on her face. She smelled like furniture polish.

"I'm so glad to see you, Chelsea! Robin hit Jeanna for some reason and gave her a bloody nose. Now Robin won't speak to anyone. And Jeanna won't either."

"I'll talk to Robin."

"Thanks. You seem to be the only one who can get a response from her."

Chelsea smiled. "I want to help her. I like her."

"She's in the family room again."

Chelsea hurried to the family room. She found

Robin at a table filled with materials. She didn't look up or smile at Chelsea like she usually did.

"Is something wrong, Robin?" Chelsea asked softly.

Robin sniffed hard and shook her head.

Chelsea sighed and sat across the table from her. She could tell Robin was close to tears and would be really really embarrassed if she burst out crying. Sunlight streamed through the windows behind the table. "Let's work on the macramé owls," Chelsea said as brightly as she could. "Did you get the branch for the owl to sit on?"

Her shoulders drooping, Robin kept her head down.

Just then Jeanna peeked around a chair where she'd been hiding. "Robin's such a baby!"

Robin's flaming red head shot up, and she glared at Jeanna. "Just shut up!" Robin leaped up and rushed at Jeanna.

Chelsea caught her and held her thin body tightly. Robin kicked and struggled, and Chelsea held her tighter. "Stop it, Robin! I'll leave if you don't quit!"

Immediately Robin stopped, then quietly sat down. Finally she picked up her yarn and started to work on her owl.

Chelsea relaxed and slowly walked around the table and stopped beside Jeanna.

Jeanna puckered up her face as if she were going to cry.

Chelsea sat down on the chair and pulled Jeanna beside her. "Want to tell me what's wrong?

Jeanna nodded. "It's my fault," she whispered close to Chelsea's ear. "I took Robin's stick for her owl. I'm really sorry."

Chelsea smiled and squeezed Jeanna's shoulder. "Why don't you tell Robin that and give the stick back?"

Jeanna's face turned brick-red. "I . . . I broke it."

"Oh! Well, then, why don't you find another one for her?"

Jeanna's face lit up. "Should I?"

"Yes." Chelsea hugged Jeanna. "And tell her you're sorry."

Slowly Jeanna walked around the table to Robin. "I really am sorry I broke your stick. I'll find another one for you."

Robin's eyes widened in surprise, and she rubbed her hands on her jeans.

"I can find a good one for you. Honest!" Jeanna smiled, and finally Robin did too.

Chelsea sat very still as she watched the two girls. Finally Jeanna ran out to find a stick, saying she'd be back soon.

Robin worked quietly, tying the knots to turn

73

the yarn into a macramé owl to use as a wall hanging.

"I sent in our entry request and fee," Chelsea said softly.

Robin looked up with a glad laugh. "You did? I was afraid I'd dreamed it all."

"You didn't."

"Sometimes I dream stuff I think is real. But Mom told me I was having nightmares." Robin bit her lip, and a haunted look crossed her face. "I'd hurt bad like it was real. Can nightmares hurt you?"

Chelsea frowned. "You mean, give you bruises? That kind of hurt?"

Robin barely nodded her head.

Chelsea locked her hands in her lap. Silently she prayed for the right words. "Nightmares can't leave bruises, even though they're scary. But sometimes real things happen that are so terrible we don't want to remember them. Could that be what happened to you?"

"Mom says it wasn't." Robin rubbed a hand over her eyes. "She wouldn't lie to me, would she?"

Before Chelsea could answer, Jeanna ran into the room, a stick in her hand. She smiled, and her eyes sparkled. "Look, Robin, it's even better than the other one."

"Thanks," Robin whispered. Then she smiled at Jeanna. "It is a perfect stick. Want to watch me make my owl?"

"Sure!" Jeanna sat beside Robin and watched.

Chelsea knew Robin wouldn't say anything more about what had happened to her—not now. Chelsea bit back a sigh, then helped Robin untangle the yarn.

That night Chelsea walked across her bedroom that was lit only by the moonlight and opened the door. A dim light burned in the hallway. She pulled her robe around her as she walked past Rob's closed door and down the stairs. Everyone was asleep, and she should be too. The cricket Dad had been trying to get rid of for weeks sang from somewhere close. The house creaked. She stopped beside Dad's favorite chair and wished she would've told her family what Robin had said. She'd excused herself from dinner in a strangled voice, and Mom had looked at her with questions in her eyes. Chelsea shook her head and gripped the back of the chair. What was she going to do? She'd prayed for Robin—prayed the pain she'd experienced would go away—prayed she'd tell what had happened to her so she could get help.

Chelsea walked toward the kitchen and bumped against the coffee table with her bare foot. Her toe throbbed, and she clutched it and bit back a cry of pain. Finally she hobbled to the kitchen and turned on the light above the stove. Maybe a glass of milk would help her sleep. She opened the refrigerator, lifted out the jug of milk, and filled a small glass. She sat at the table and wrapped her hands around the cold glass.

Just then Rob peeked around the kitchen door with a sheepish grin. He had on the gray sweats he often wore as pajamas. "Hi, Chelsea. Can I join you?"

"Sure. What are you doing up?"

"I couldn't sleep." He pulled out a chair and sat down with a sigh.

"You never have trouble sleeping."

Rob shot her a look. "How do you know?"

Chelsea frowned thoughtfully. "I guess I don't really know. I've been so busy with everything, I haven't noticed what's going on with you."

"It's Nick Rand. I think he stole my computer game and is working on it with Jimmy Daniels."

"That's awful!"

"I don't know what to do."

Chelsea slowly rubbed a finger around the rim of her glass. "I don't either. Have you talked to him?"

Rob shook his head. "I guess I was afraid of what he'd say."

"Ask anyway! Maybe there's something else keeping him away. You know how Nick's mom is. Maybe she wouldn't let him go anywhere. She did that before. It embarrasses Nick to say anything."

Rob sighed. "I'd forgotten about his mom. You could be right."

Chelsea grinned. "I sometimes am."

"I know." Rob narrowed his eyes. "How's it going with Joan Golnek?"

"Okay."

"I heard she got in trouble again in P.E."

Chelsea's eyes widened, and her face turned as white as the milk in her glass. "What kind of trouble?"

"She hit a girl—gave her a black eye. I sure don't want her to hurt you."

Chelsea swallowed hard. "I wonder why Joan acts the way she does."

Rob shrugged.

"I think I'll find out."

"And I'll find out what's going on with Nick."

Chelsea drained the glass of milk and dabbed her mouth with a white paper napkin. "I think we'd better both get back to bed."

"I'm glad we talked, Chel."

"It has been a while, hasn't it?" Chelsea rinsed her glass and set it in the sink. "Let me know what happens with Nick."

"I will. And you be careful of Joan."

A shiver trickled down Chelsea's spine. "I will. Believe me, I will."

The Truth About Robin

On Friday, between English and gym, Chelsea hurried to the girls' restroom. None of the Best Friends could go with her, but she was sure after her talk with Joan last Saturday that she'd be all right alone. Joan hadn't bothered her at all the past three days.

Chelsea pushed the door open. Treva stood at the mile-long mirror brushing her hair. She glanced toward the door, then frowned.

Chelsea wanted to back out, but she stepped inside and let the door close behind her. The bathroom smelled like soap and perfume. Her yellow sweater and new jeans felt too warm.

With her eyes narrowed, Treva faced Chelsea squarely. "You'd better tell Joan Golnek to leave me alone."

Chelsea's stomach tightened. What had Joan done this time? "Tell her yourself."

"I have, but she won't listen to me!"

"What makes you think she'll listen to me?" Chelsea inched toward the first stall.

"She's a troublemaker, you know. I can't believe you want to help her with anything."

Chelsea shrugged.

Treva shook her finger at Chelsea. "Stay away from Joan! It's not your business to help her."

With her jaw set stubbornly, Chelsea stepped toward Treva. "I will help Joan Golnek if I want! And I'll see her if I want, when I want."

Surprised, Treva stumbled back. "Well, you don't have to get mad! I was going to tell everyone to buy your crafts. I sure won't now!"

"I don't need your help! I'll sell my work because it's good!"

"Oh no, you won't! Nobody will buy it. You'll see. I'll make sure of that, especially if you try to help Joan."

"I'll help Joan no matter what you say."

"You'll be sorry!" Treva ran out, slamming the door behind her.

Chelsea snickered. She would not be afraid of Treva ever again! Chelsea flipped back her red hair. Why on earth didn't Treva want her to help Joan? "Well, I'm going to!" In fact, she'd set a definite time to get together with Joan that very day!

For the rest of the school day Chelsea looked for Joan but never saw her. Maybe she'd stayed home. She told the Best Friends about Treva's warning. They said they'd help find Joan. And they said they'd spread the word about Chelsea's fantastic crafts.

After school Chelsea wolfed down an apple, then picked up the kitchen telephone and called Joan. There was no answer. Slowly Chelsea hung up the receiver and leaned against the kitchen counter. Where was Joan? It felt strange not to have her around like she had been the past two weeks.

Rob walked into the kitchen. "Why the long face?"

Chelsea flipped her hair over her shoulder. "I've been trying to call Joan, but there's no answer. She wasn't in school today."

"Her brother wasn't either."

"Maybe they went on a vacation or something."

Rob shrugged. "It's a funny time to go on vacation. Thanksgiving vacation is coming soon."

"I know." Chelsea shrugged. "Oh well, I'll try later. I have to get to the church." She hurried to her bedroom. It was overflowing with crafts that she'd set out for the table at the Arts and Crafts Show. Ever since she was eight years old she'd been making things for her own enjoyment and to give away as gifts. She touched a red velvet squirrel she'd made just last year. It was in the pile of things to sell, and so was a tiny squirrel that she'd made from a cotton ball and some yarn.

She touched a black and white skunk and a tiny pink bunny. She slipped Sammy onto her hand and giggled. Soon the clutter would be gone from her room and would be on display in the show. How much would be sold, and how much would she carry back home? she wondered.

Would Joan come to the show?

Chelsea shook her head and laughed under her breath. For two weeks she'd tried to hide from Joan, and now she was trying to find her. *Lord, You do have a sense of humor, don't You.*

Chelsea glanced at the clock beside her tidy bed, then grabbed up the material for the last craft class and rushed away, calling good-bye to Rob. Hannah had said she'd meet her at the church.

Later Chelsea stepped inside the church and smiled at John Alexander, who was standing near the door. He was a freshman in college and was studying art. She knew he enjoyed teaching the kids arts and crafts and that he'd miss not having class after today as much as she would.

John grinned as he pushed his hands into the pockets of his jeans. "Are you all set for the Arts and Crafts Show?"

"Just about." Chelsea fell into step beside him as they walked toward the Sunday school wing. The smell of popcorn filled the air. A baby cried, then was quiet. "I have a few things to finish. I'm finally beginning to get excited about it."

"I'm looking forward to seeing your things. My mother goes to the shows all the time, so she'll be there. I'll tell her to find you."

"That'll be nice." Chelsea smiled at John. Since teaching together, she and John had become good friends. He was nice, and he made her laugh even when she was sure she was too tired to ever laugh again.

In the classroom she stopped at her table while John walked to his. She looked around the room to see if Robin had come yet. Today was her first day back since she'd hurt her ankle. She said she wanted to return even though it was the last day of classes. The bright red hair stood out from the browns and blondes. As Chelsea watched, Robin ran at John Alexander and kicked him hard in the shin. Surprised, he stumbled back, then grabbed Robin and shouted angrily at her.

Chelsea gasped and cried, "Don't, John!"

Robin screamed more and more loudly, and abruptly John released her. Before Chelsea could reach her, Robin sped out the door.

"Come back, Robin!" Chelsea called.

"Robin!" John pushed his trembling fingers through his dark hair. His face was red. "That girl!"

"I'm going after her," Chelsea said. "Tell Mrs. Leeds what happened and that I'll be back with Robin as soon as possible."

Chelsea ran into the hall, but Robin wasn't in

sight. She caught a glimpse of Robin's red head outside. Chelsea raced out the door and across the grass. "Robin, it's me—Chelsea! Please stop!"

But Robin raced down the sidewalk and away from the church. She ran as if she'd never had a sprained ankle.

Frantically Chelsea called again. She had to catch Robin before she twisted her ankle again or ran into traffic. Two boys shouted at her from in front of a yellow house. A dog barked at her heels. "Get away from me!" Robin shouted. The dog slunk away, its tail between its legs.

Finally Chelsea caught Robin by the arm, and they tumbled together onto the soft grass of a well-trimmed yard.

"Don't hit me!" Robin screamed as she kicked and twisted.

With a gasp of alarm Chelsea struggled to hold Robin tight. Chelsea pushed her mouth against Robin's ear and said in a gasping voice, "Stop, Robin! Stop it right now! I won't hurt you, and John won't either!"

Robin turned her head, then snapped her mouth closed and sagged against Chelsea. Robin smelled hot and sweaty.

"You're all right, Robin. No one will hurt you." Chelsea pulled Robin's tangled hair out of her face and tucked it behind her ears. "John didn't mean to get mad."

"I won't go back," Robin whispered brokenly as she lifted her tear-stained face to Chelsea.

"We must go back. Mrs. Leeds will be worried. But when we get back, she'll call your parents so they can pick you up and take you home."

"No . . . no!"

Chelsea caught Robin's flailing hands and held them firmly. "You're all right, Robin. John didn't hurt you. He got mad and yelled at you because you kicked him."

A shadow fell across the grass, and Chelsea looked up to find John standing there with a grief-stricken look on his face. She shook her head slightly, and he backed away, his hands stuffed into his jeans pockets, his broad shoulders slumped dejectedly.

"I hate him," Robin whispered hoarsely. "He beat me!"

Chelsea shook her head. "John didn't beat you, Robin. I was watching, and he didn't. Look!" Chelsea pointed to Robin's arms. "You don't have any bruises."

Robin's hazel eyes grew big and round. "Not John, Chelsea. Ray Flood! He beat me so hard! But Mom said it was only a nightmare!" Robin shivered and gripped Chelsea more tightly.

"Ray Flood isn't here now, Robin."

Robin shivered. "He got mad at me because I wouldn't leave the house when he wanted to be

84

alone with Mom. But I didn't leave! I didn't want him to be alone with Mom. He was awful! He said I was rotten and stubborn and mean, and I kicked him twice on the leg. He yelled at me and slugged me and then just kept beating me." Tears gushed from Robin's eyes, and her slight shoulders shook with ragged sobs. "I know it happened! Mom was wrong! It wasn't a nightmare."

Chelsea's stomach churned, and a bitter taste filled her mouth. She clung to Robin and rubbed her back and prayed softly for her.

Finally Robin pulled away and knuckled away her tears.

"Robin, your life is different now." Chelsea wiped tears from Robin's freckled cheeks. "The Osborns don't beat you. Ray Flood isn't around. You live with a wonderful family, and they love you a lot."

"They pray for me," Robin whispered, her eyes wide.

"I know. I do too, Robin. We know God loves you and wants you to have a good life with a loving family."

Robin ducked her head.

"Let's go back to the church now."

Robin gulped. "If you're sure nobody will hurt me."

"I'm sure." Chelsea motioned to John. "Our friend John came to take us back in his car."

John cleared his throat as he squatted down beside Robin. "I'm really sorry for getting mad at you."

"I didn't mean to kick you," Robin whispered.

John rubbed his shin and laughed. "And I didn't mean to yell at you. I'll never do it again."

Robin studied John intently, then turned to Chelsea with a questioning look on her face.

"He won't," Chelsea said softly.

"My car's over there." John pointed to a small red sedan. "Let's go."

Robin slowly stood, then ran to the car and sat in the backseat.

John shot a relieved look at Chelsea.

"It's going to be all right, John."

"I hope so. I can't believe I lost control."

Chelsea squeezed his hand. She was thankful she'd finally learned the truth about Robin.

Back at the church Robin walked between John and Chelsea, holding their hands. She was quiet and subdued. Maybe now the Osborns could convince her they cared.

Mrs. Leeds met them in the hall and listened to their story. She smiled at Robin. "I'm glad you're all right. Would you like to go home?"

Robin shook her head. She looked up at Chelsea. "Do I have to?"

"No. You're welcome to stay."

"Then I'll stay."

Mrs. Leeds smiled. "Good. We'd better get inside and get our projects under way."

Chelsea smiled and followed the others into the room.

7

The Phone Call

On Friday night Joan Golnek walked listlessly through the small dimly lit house. Outside it was a rundown dump, but inside she kept the shabby furniture and rooms clean. Nobody else seemed to care, but she did! She would not live in a dirty mess! Shivering, she pulled her sweater closer to herself. Dad hadn't paid the gas bill again, so there was no heat.

The phone rang, and she jumped, then ran to answer it. She was home alone—as usual. The only phone in the house was in the living room. She hesitated. Was it Mom saying she was coming back? Trembling, Joan bit her lip. What would she say if it were Mom? When she'd left, she said she'd made a big mistake marrying a man who couldn't provide for his own family. But that was really only an excuse to leave. She wanted freedom from responsibility—Joan knew that for a fact. Her hands icy, she picked up the receiver and sank to the sagging brown sofa. "Hello."

"This is Chelsea McCrea."

Joan's eyes widened, and she bit back a gasp. McCrea was calling her! It was too good to be true! McCrea sounded different—like she was talking with her mouth full. Why had she called? Maybe she was calling to say she'd changed her mind. Joan's heart sank. "Yeah, McCrea, what do you want?" Joan gripped the receiver so hard, her knuckles hurt.

"I was stupid to ever agree to teach you! I won't do it, and I won't even talk to you again as long as I live!" She hung up with a slam.

Trembling, Joan dropped the receiver in place. She sat in stunned silence a long time. "I'll show her! She can't . . . can't do this to . . . me!" Joan burst into wild sobs and flung herself facedown on the sofa.

Much later she sat up, blew her nose, and wiped her eyes. Her throat and head ached. She flung Dad's newspaper to the floor and kicked it, scattering it around the small room.

The door opened, and Hank walked in. He frowned. "What in the world are you doing?"

"Nothing!" Joan crossed her arms and dropped to the sofa.

"Dad's gonna have a fit."

"So?"

Hank picked up the newspaper and refolded it. The noise of rustling paper filled the room for a long time. At last Hank dropped the folded paper on Dad's chair. Hank sank to the sofa and twisted around to face Joan. "You sick?"

"No. I'm mad!"

"How come?"

Joan rubbed her nose with the back of her hand. "McCrea won't teach me photography."

"What else is new?"

"But she said she would! She promised, but then she called a while ago and said she wouldn't."

Hank brushed his tangled hair back. "That don't sound like McCrea."

"She's not as nice as we thought."

"What are you gonna do about it?"

Joan narrowed her eyes and doubled her fists. "I don't know, but I'll think of something." She'd thought she could trust McCrea. She'd asked her to call her Chelsea!

"Why didn't you call her right back and tell her off?"

She shrugged. She'd been too upset to talk without crying. There was no way she'd let McCrea or anyone hear her cry!

Just then the door opened, and Dad walked in, his face haggard. He pulled off his cap and rubbed a hand over his thick brown hair. "Why's it so cold in here?"

"You didn't pay the gas bill," Hank said tiredly.

Dad grabbed up his newspaper and slapped it

hard against his hand. "What a jerk! I'm sure sorry, kids. It's hard to remember all them details."

Joan sighed. "I told you I could pay the bills. I did it for Mom."

"You're just a little girl." Dad clamped a hand on Joan's shoulder, then eased down in his chair. "I don't want you stuck with payin' bills."

"So you'd rather be cold?"

Dad chuckled.

"She's right, Dad," Hank said.

"I really can do it." Joan pulled her feet up under her and faced Dad. "You leave the money, and I'll take the bill and the money and pay it. I did it for Mom all the time."

Dad scowled. "I'm real sorry, Joannie. If I didn't have two jobs, I'd remember to take care of them things."

Joan forced back tears. As soon as she could, she'd learn photography so she could sell her work and help with the bills. She knew she could do better work than some she'd seen in the newspaper. Her heart sank. McCrea had said she wouldn't teach her. And nobody else would either—she'd already asked. Besides, it would cost too much to learn from someone else or to join the Photography Club. She hated McCrea!

"What's wrong, Joannie?"

"She's just tired," Hank said before Joan could speak.

Joan dropped her feet to the floor. Hank always tried to protect Dad from problems of any kind—big or small.

"Get to bed then." Dad yawned. "Anything to eat?"

"Not much. A little milk and a can of soup are the only things in the house. Give me some money and I'll get some groceries tomorrow," Joan offered.

Dad yawned and stood up. "I'll go now. Want to come, Hank?"

"Sure." Hank jumped up.

"You get to bed, Joan." Dad patted Joan's shoulder. "Cover up warm. I'll leave the money to pay the gas bill."

"I'll take care of it." Joan smiled weakly. Could she sleep knowing she had no chance of making money to help with the bills?

She watched Dad and Hank walk out, then paced the house again. She stopped at the front window and looked out at the darkness. "I'll get you, McCrea!"

■

At The Ravines the Best Friends sat on Hannah's bed and laughed at a joke Kathy had told. Hannah's three little sisters giggled from their beds across the room. The entire basement was a bedroom and playroom for the four girls. They even had their own bathroom and a huge closet. And they were far enough from Baby Burke's room to not be awakened by his crying in the night.

When it was quiet again, Roxie turned to Chelsea. "Give me the information about my *King's Kids* job tomorrow. I had it on the refrigerator, but Lacy threw it away when she was cleaning." Roxie sighed and shook her head. "My sister is a neatnic!"

Chelsea opened the notebook she kept all the calls in for *King's Kids*. She was president of the business because she'd started it to make money to pay a phone bill she'd built up by calling her best friend back in Oklahoma. Others had wanted to earn money too, so she'd let them in on the business. They were called *King's Kids* because Jesus was their King and they all belonged to Him. "Give Roxie a pencil and paper, Hannah, so she can write it down."

Hannah pulled a small notebook and stubby yellow pencil out of her nightstand drawer and handed them to Roxie.

"The address is 3890 Ash Street. That's not very far from here. Madalynn Eldred is the woman who called. She wants you to decorate the basement for Candi's birthday party. She's going to be five. Mrs. Eldred has all the decorations. She wants you there by 1. The party is at 4."

Roxie wrinkled her nose. "I'm not very good at decorating."

Hannah hugged her stuffed bunny. "Candi is

sooo cute! I baby-sat for her last week. And Mrs. Eldred never forgets to pay."

"I'm glad she doesn't want me to stay to help with the party." Roxie stuffed the folded paper into the front pocket of her jeans.

Chelsea yawned. "I'd better get home. I have to take Mike to the park again in the morning—unless it's raining. Or snowing." She shivered at the thought. She didn't like cold weather and wasn't looking forward to her first Michigan winter. Mike, of course, couldn't wait to build snowmen, roll in the snow, and go sledding and ice-skating.

"We're going with you to the park," Hannah said. She grinned at Kathy, who was staying the night. "We won't talk too late, will we?"

"We told your mom we wouldn't. We don't want to keep the little girls awake."

"We don't mind," the twins said.

Lena giggled. "We like to listen to what you say."

Chelsea picked up her jacket and notebook and headed for the stairs with Roxie behind her. "Bye, everyone."

"Keep the noise down so we don't hear you across the street." Roxie laughed.

"Good night," the girls all said together.

A few minutes later Chelsea waved to Roxie and ran into her house. Music drifted in from the living room. Mom was in the kitchen drinking a cup of tea and jotting something in a notebook. "Hi, Mom."

She looked up and smiled. "Hi, hon. Want some tea?"

"No, thanks." Chelsea hung her jacket in the closet and walked to the table. "Did Joan call?"

Mom shook her head. "But Peter Stone did."

Chelsea scowled. "What did he want?"

"He didn't say. Said he'd talk to you tomorrow."

"I wonder what he wants."

"I asked if he'd like to leave a message, but he didn't." Mom shrugged. "It sounded like a girl in the background was telling him what to say."

"Probably Treva. Peter does *everything* she tells him to do!"

"That's too bad. One of these days they'll end up being enemies. True friends never force each other to do things they don't want to do."

Chelsea thought about Joan. "You're right, Mom." Chelsea kissed Mom's cheek. "See you in the morning."

"I left a Scripture on your desk."

"Thanks." Chelsea smiled. Mom did that often, and Chelsea liked it.

Slowly Chelsea walked upstairs. What on earth did Peter Stone want? And why hadn't Joan tracked her down or called her tonight? Was something wrong?

"Heavenly Father, take care of Joan tonight. Help her sleep in peace," Chelsea whispered.

8

The Search for Joan

Saturday morning Chelsea stood beside the Best Friends at the wishing well. The park rang with shouts and laughter. Some families were even having picnics—taking advantage of a perfect Indian summer day. Across the park Mike and his friends were practicing again. Mom had said they couldn't pass up two warm Saturdays in a row. Rob had a job at the corner grocery store, so once again Chelsea had been asked to baby-sit Mike. Naturally Mike wouldn't call it baby-sitting, but Chelsea knew that's what it was. Mike liked to think she was with him because she wanted to watch him practice. She did enjoy seeing him, but she would've enjoyed two additional hours of sleep even more.

Shielding her eyes against the sun, Hannah looked all around. "Do you really think Joan will show up?"

Chelsea nodded. "Yesterday was the only day she didn't hang around me. She'll be here."

"When will you start teaching her?" Kathy asked.

"One week from today is the Arts and Crafts Show. So I plan to teach her after school the following Monday—if she can do it then." Chelsea frowned. "I'd sure like to know why Treva is mad just because I'm planning to help Joan."

Hannah shook her head. "I can't figure it out. I didn't know the girls even knew each other enough to be enemies."

Kathy giggled. "Joan's everybody's enemy."

"Peter Stone might know," Roxie said thoughtfully. "We could ask him."

"Great idea." Hannah patted Roxie on the back. "Except I already thought of that and asked him—he said he didn't know."

Roxie made a face at Hannah. "We can't all be super-sleuths with minds like steel traps."

The Best Friends laughed.

"Maybe Peter lied." Kathy raised her brows questioningly.

"He could've." Chelsea nodded. "I say let's go to Joan's home and talk to her." Chelsea glanced at the Best Friends with her hand high. "Who votes yes?"

"I do!" they all said at once as they raised their hands.

Later the Best Friends rode their bikes to Joan's house. It was a bad part of town, but they'd promised their parents they'd stay together. They laid their bikes on the ground and ran to the front door. Rock music blared from the house next door. Across the street several girls played keepaway with a basketball on the sidewalk.

Chelsea knocked a tiny rap, giggled, then knocked again—harder this time.

Hank opened the door. He was fourteen, tall, and toothpick-thin. The smell of hot chocolate and the blare of the TV drifted out around him. He scowled. "What do you want?"

His rude tone startled Chelsea. She swallowed hard. "I came to see Joan." Chelsea glanced past Hank just in time to see Joan duck out of sight.

Hank started to shut the door. "She's not here."

Roxie stuck her foot in the door. "We saw her."

Hank pushed his face close to Roxie's. "You calling me a liar?"

Hannah tugged on Roxie.

Chelsea shivered. "We want to talk to Joan. I have an important message for her."

"Too bad!" Hank slammed the door.

Chelsea gasped as she faced the Best Friends. "I don't understand . . . Why wouldn't Joan talk to me?"

Kathy shrugged. "Maybe she's embarrassed

that we're here—what with her rundown house and all."

Hannah tapped her finger against her chin. "It doesn't make sense. Joan has been your shadow for two weeks. Why not now?"

"I sure don't know." Chelsea walked slowly to her bike. "We can't break the door down, so we might as well go home."

Chelsea's mind whirled with frantic thoughts as she followed the Best Friends back to The Ravines. They stopped in her yard and looked at each other. Down the street kids played noisily in their yard. Gracie barked and ran down the sidewalk toward home. Chelsea moved from one foot to the other.

"Very strange," Hannah said softly. "Something's going on . . . And I am going to find out what."

Kathy frowned. "How? Joan won't talk to us."

"I'd like to help, but I have to eat lunch and get to the Eldreds'." Roxie made a face. "To decorate."

"Want me to help?" Kathy asked.

Chelsea shook her head. "Mrs. Eldred asked for only one. She said two would just get in each other's way."

Kathy shrugged. "Or maybe she didn't want to pay for two. That happens a lot, you know."

"I guess you can ask. She's a good customer and won't drop us." Chelsea laid her bike beside the garage. "See you all later."

After eating a grilled cheese sandwich and a dill pickle for lunch, Chelsea rode her bike to Robin's house. She stopped near the porch, then frowned thoughtfully. She was a little early. She'd see Peter Stone first.

Her stomach knotted as she pedaled to Peter's house. It was a two-story white frame house with green shutters and a wide front screened-in porch. She'd heard it had been built by Peter's great-great-grandfather, a lumber baron in the 1800s.

Chelsea took a deep breath. Dare she knock on the door and ask for Peter?

Just then she heard a noise at the side of the house. Peter was lying on his stomach with his camera focused on something in the grass. Chelsea crept up to him and squatted beside him. "What is it?" she whispered.

"A caterpillar." His voice was low and tense, and he didn't look at her.

She bent down and finally spotted it on a leaf. It was two shades of brown and was very fuzzy.

He clicked the camera, then clicked again.

Just then the screen door slammed.

With a gasp Peter leaped up and thrust his camera into Chelsea's hand. His face was pale. He took a deep breath and forced himself to relax.

"What's wrong?" Chelsea whispered.

"My dad," Peter said out of the side of his mouth.

With a bag of golf clubs over his shoulder, Mr. Stone strode over to them, the sunlight making his hair look almost white-blond. He wore golfing pants and shirt. He scowled at the camera, then smiled at Chelsea. "Hello."

"Hi," she said in a small voice.

"Dad, this is Chelsea McCrea. Her family comes from Oklahoma."

"It's nice to meet you." He motioned to the camera in her hand. "I see you're interested in photography."

Chelsea nodded.

"She's one of the best in the club." Peter smiled at Chelsea.

"Is that so?"

"Peter's very good too." Chelsea smiled at Peter. She saw the sudden fear in his eyes. Was he afraid she'd reveal that the camera was his? She turned back to Mr. Stone. "I like taking pictures."

Mr. Stone eased his clubs to the ground beside him. "I'm glad Peter's not that involved. He has more important things to do."

"Sure do." Peter's voice sounded hollow.

Mr. Stone hoisted his bag back into place. "I must be going. Nice to meet you, Chelsea." He looked intently at Peter, then motioned to the basketball hoop beside the garage. "Craig said he'll be out later."

Peter nodded.

Chelsea felt the tension in him as they watched Mr. Stone drive away.

"Craig's my big brother—the one who's great in every sport. Dad's determined that I'll be just like him."

Chelsea slowly handed back the camera. "I hope the photo of the caterpillar turns out good."

Peter smiled. "Thanks for your help. I couldn't handle having Dad yell at me again. He blows up when he sees me with a camera."

"I'm sorry."

"Yeah, me too." Peter let out his breath. "I'll show you the picture when I get it developed."

"Thanks. I'd like to see it. I took one of a ladybug that turned out great."

"Show me sometime, would you?"

"Sure." Chelsea glanced at her watch. "Oh, it's late. I gotta get to Robin's. Talk to you later."

Peter nodded.

When she walked toward her bike, Peter ran after her. "Chelsea, wait a minute."

She saw the strained look on his face. She lifted her brow questioningly.

A muscle jumped in his jaw. "Aw, nothing. See ya around."

"See ya." Frowning in thought, she pedaled to Robin's. What had Peter started to say? Suddenly she remembered she hadn't asked why he'd called last night. She'd have to ask later.

She ran onto the Osborns' porch and knocked on the door.

Robin flung the door wide and pulled Chelsea inside. "Wait'll you see what I made!"

Chelsea laughed. It was wonderful to see Robin so excited.

Robin stopped in the family room and with a wide flourish of her arm pointed to a floppy-legged boy doll with brown string hair, striped bibbed overalls, and a big nose that made Chelsea laugh.

Chelsea picked it up. "It's great! So original! Somebody will love this! Especially people who collect country crafts. I'd like to show him to my mom."

"Take him if you want. You could bring him back when you come next time."

"Thanks!"

"I don't know if I want to sell him."

"I know how you feel." Grinning, Chelsea studied the boy doll in great detail, then finally set him back in place. "Did you finish the owl?"

Robin wrinkled her nose. "I had to put it aside for a while. It sometimes gets boring to tie all those knots."

"I know. But it's worth it when you create something interesting." Chelsea sat at the table and once again picked up the boy doll. "This is really great, Robin!"

"Thanks." She looked ready to burst with pride.

Two hours later Chelsea took the boy doll and pedaled home. She'd show Mom the doll, put it in her room, then check with Hannah to see what was new with Joan.

Chelsea frowned. Why wouldn't Joan talk to her this morning? It just didn't make sense. "Heavenly Father, show Joan that You love her."

9

The Missing Crafts

Shivering, Joan stopped outside the McCreas' front door. Last night she'd stayed awake until she'd decided on the perfect plan to get even with McCrea. It would work better than any other plan—even better than a bloody nose.

Joan rang the doorbell, then moved restlessly. A dog barked, and she jumped nervously. A pickup drove past.

Mrs. McCrea opened the door. The smell of furniture polish drifted out. "Hello, Joan. Did Chelsea find you?"

Find her? Joan forced a smile. "Hi, Mrs. McCrea. Is she home?" Joan couldn't bring herself to say *Chelsea*. Joan locked her hands together behind her back. She knew Chelsea was across the street at Hannah Shigwam's.

"She's at the Shigwams'. Go over to see her. I know she wants to talk to you."

Joan pulled two large red buttons from the pocket of her jeans and held them out. "She wanted these for her crafts. Can I leave them in her room?"

"Sure. Go right on up." Mrs. McCrea held the door wide. "I'll be in my study if you need me."

Joan hesitated, then hurried to the open stairs. She'd never lived in a house with an upstairs. Her legs trembled, but she walked up the steps without stumbling.

In Chelsea's room she looked at the two piles of crafts. Some of the things really were cute, though most of them were too babyish for her. She brushed her tangled hair off her cheeks as she gazed around the room. McCrea had her own phone! A boy doll with a big nose sat on the desk near it. Joan picked up the doll. "It must be special to be sitting here." She dropped it facedown on the desk beside the two red buttons.

She ducked out into the hall and opened what she hoped was the linen closet. It was. She needed a sheet to wrap the crafts in. There were too many crafts for one sheet, so she pulled out two. She held her breath and listened. Mrs. McCrea wasn't coming to check on her. How'd Mrs. McCrea know she wasn't stealing everything in sight? She frowned. She didn't steal! But stories around school were that she did—and that she did drugs and a lot of other terrible things. Maybe Mrs. McCrea hadn't heard any of the bad stories.

In the bedroom Joan spread out a sheet, tossed one pile of crafts on it, then tied the corners together. She started to push the bundle under Chelsea's bed, then stopped. She laughed under her breath. She'd hide them in Rob's room. McCrea would blame him! "Good plan," Joan whispered.

Joan half-dragged, half-carried the bundle to a bedroom across the hall. The toys and gymnastics trophies let her know it was Mike's room. Carefully she lifted the bedspread and pushed the bundle under it, then dashed back for the next pile. She pushed it under the bed in Rob's room. She touched his computer, longing for one for Hank. Maybe she'd talk Hank into learning computer so he could help make money for the family. Maybe someday they could live in a nice house and have nice clothes. Maybe someday Dad could work only one job instead of two. Joan sighed and pushed away her daydreams that she was sure would never come true.

Back in Chelsea's room she grabbed up the boy doll. Should she take it home with her? She shook her head. If anyone stopped her, she didn't want any evidence on her. She carried the chair to the closet, jumped up on it, and hid the doll on the top shelf behind a pile of boxes. Her heart racing, she put the chair back, dusted off her hands, and said, "There. Now we're even."

Joan ran lightly downstairs, took a deep steadying breath, and poked her head into the study. "I'm going now."

Mrs. McCrea looked up with a smile. "Oh, I thought you'd left already. Bye."

"That's sure a cute doll by your daughter's phone."

"I know. I love it!"

"I put the buttons beside it."

"Good. I'll tell Chelsea. But you'll probably see her first, so you tell her."

"Sure . . . Okay." Smiling, Joan lifted her hand in a wave.

Mrs. McCrea tucked a strand of red hair behind her ear. "I'm glad Chelsea's going to help you with photography. She's a good teacher."

Joan's smile wavered. Didn't Mrs. McCrea know about the terrible phone call? "I gotta go. Bye."

"Bye, hon."

Her eyes smarting with tears, Joan ran from the house to her bike. She darted a look at the Shigwams' but didn't see anyone. She pedaled quickly away, her heart hammering.

Mrs. McCrea had called her *hon*. Mom never had! And Mrs. McCrea had trusted her to go to Chelsea's room alone. Mom never trusted Joan in *her* bedroom. Mom had always been afraid Joan would steal her change or her cigarettes.

Just as Joan pedaled past a yellow house with white shutters Roxie and Kathy walked out.

"Joan!" they called happily.

Joan's heart zoomed to her feet. She thought about racing away, but she stopped and turned to them. "Hi."

"Did you see Chelsea?" Kathy asked excitedly.

"She wants to set up a time to meet with you," Roxie said.

Joan frowned. "If McCrea wants me, she can find me."

"We all were at your house this morning." Roxie stepped closer to Joan. "We know you were home."

"Why wouldn't you talk to us?" Kathy frowned. "Wouldn't your brother let you?"

"What does it matter?"

Kathy's smile faltered, then she said brightly, "You won't believe what we were just doing!"

"What?" Joan wanted to snatch back the question, but it was too late.

"Decorating for a birthday party." Roxie rolled her eyes. "We never dreamed it would take so long."

"Why'd you do it if you didn't like it?"

"It was a *King's Kids* job." Kathy pushed the sleeves of her sweater up. "One of the rules is to finish a job we promised to do."

Roxie pointed at Joan. "Hey, you might like to be part of *King's Kids*."

Joan frowned. "I don't know what you're talking about."

Roxie and Kathy told Joan about the business and how it had come into being.

"It's a great way to make money," Kathy said. "That way we can buy our own school clothes and things like that."

Joan's heart leaped. She did want to be a *King's Kid*. She scowled. What was she thinking? She didn't want to even be in the same state with McCrea after what she'd done! "I gotta get home to make supper." Joan pedaled quickly away. What was going on? Why were the girls so nice to her? And why didn't McCrea's mom and friends know McCrea had refused to help her or even speak to her again?

Roxie shook her head as she watched Joan ride out of sight. "She's really strange."

"Maybe she decided she didn't want to learn to take pictures." Kathy sighed tiredly. "I didn't know decorating for a birthday party could be so hard or take so long."

"I'm sure glad Mrs. Eldred said you could help me. I'd never have gotten done before the party if you hadn't."

"I know." Kathy walked to her bike. "Let's go see Chelsea and Hannah. Maybe Hannah has this case solved."

Roxie giggled. "Sure. I bet she does."

"I wonder why Joan was on our street but wouldn't stop to see Chelsea?" Kathy straddled her bike.

A few minutes later they sat on Hannah's deck, and Kathy asked Hannah and Chelsea the same question.

Chelsea shook her head. "I don't understand it at all. First Joan threatens me if I don't help her and now she won't even talk to me."

Kathy jumped up. "I say let's forget about Joan for now and play a game. I vote for Clue!" Kathy loved playing board games, especially Clue.

"I'll get it, and we'll play out here." Hannah ran inside for the game.

Chelsea chewed her bottom lip as she looked out across the backyard. Finally she turned to Roxie and Kathy. "Why was Joan on our street if she didn't come to see me?"

They shrugged.

"My brain is programmed to solve Clue only." Kathy giggled. "But keep thinking about Joan, and then I'll have a better chance to win."

Roxie jabbed Kathy's arm. "You usually win anyway. Either you or Hannah."

Chelsea wrapped her arms around her knees. "It's really strange Joan wouldn't talk to me. Really strange."

Laughing, Kathy grabbed Chelsea and shook

her. "Hey, you, you're supposed to forget about Joan for a while."

Chelsea giggled and pulled away. "All right. I guess I can for now."

Hannah rushed out of the house with the game box in one hand and a giant bag of tortilla chips in the other. "Chel, your mom just called to see if Joan stopped over."

"No kidding!"

"Your mom said Joan was there to give you something for your crafts."

Chelsea sighed in relief. "I guess she's not mad at me after all." She rubbed her hands together. "Come on, let's play! I think I'm going to win for once!"

10

Chelsea to the Rescue

Yawning, Chelsea walked into her bedroom, then stopped in surprise. All the crafts were gone! "Mom probably got tired of them on the floor and packed them away." Chelsea yawned again. She'd ask her. All at once Chelsea felt too tired to go back downstairs. Tomorrow would be soon enough.

Sunday morning Chelsea jumped out of bed and quickly dressed for church. She'd overslept! She didn't remember to ask about the crafts. She thought about it Sunday afternoon, but Mom was taking a nap, so she didn't bother her.

Outdoors Chelsea zipped up her light jacket against the chilly wind and wheeled her bike from the garage. She was baby-sitting Robin, Jeanna, and Bob this afternoon. Robin was anxious for Chelsea to see another puppet she'd made.

Chelsea waved to Hannah, who was getting in the station wagon with her family to visit friends.

Because Joan was no longer a threat, Chelsea knew it was safe for her to go alone to Robin's. Maybe afterward she'd even visit Peter to find out why he'd called Friday night. He might have his photos developed so she could see them, especially the caterpillar pictures.

As Chelsea drew close to the Osborns' she saw a small gray car driving slowly along the street. She shivered, then frowned. She wasn't sure why the car made her apprehensive. Somebody was probably just out for a Sunday drive and going slow so they could see the nice homes and yards. But she shivered again.

The car drove to the next cross street and turned right. Chelsea sighed in relief, rested her bike against the garage, and ran to the back door. Gwen Osborn let her in.

"We'll be back in about two hours." She sounded hurried. She looked over her shoulder and called, "Coming, Mel? We'll be late if we don't go now."

Robin dashed into the kitchen and caught Chelsea's hand. "Wait'll you see the puppet! Jeanna loves it!"

Mrs. Osborn pointed to the refrigerator. "The phone number of where we'll be is on that paper. The kids can have a snack after a while. They can play outdoors but can't ride their bikes."

Chelsea nodded. She felt as breathless as Mrs. Osborn sounded.

A few minutes later Chelsea stood in the family room while Robin showed her a shaggy dog puppet. Chelsea put it on her hand and laughed in delight. "It's sooo cute!"

"Let me try it on again." Bob reached for it.

Chelsea turned to Robin. "Is it all right?"

"Sure."

Bob slipped it on while Robin and Jeanna put others on. Chelsea excused herself and hurried to the living room to look out the window just as the gray car stopped across the street from the Osborns'. A woman got out of the passenger side. She had long, flowing red hair and wore jeans, a yellow shirt, and a loose-fitting yellow jacket. A man was driving. He rolled his window down to say something to the woman.

Chelsea slid the window open and listened closely.

"You get her and meet me around the corner."

"I will, Ray, but you stay out of sight. You know she's scared to death of you."

"She's got no reason to be."

"We know that, but she has this crazy notion that you beat her."

Chelsea trembled. Were they talking about Robin? Was it possible the woman was Robin's mother and the man Ray Flood? Surely not! If so, they wouldn't try to take Robin, would they?

Silently Chelsea prayed to know what to do.

The woman turned, and Chelsea jumped back, her heart hammering.

She pressed her hand to her throat. The Osborns couldn't get home soon enough to help. Who could she call? Peter Stone!

She looked up his number and quickly punched it. Her pulse raced, and sweat beaded up on her forehead. "Hurry, Peter!"

Mr. Stone answered.

"Hi. This is Chelsea. May I speak to Peter right away?"

"He's getting ready to go to the park to play ball."

"I won't keep him too long." Chelsea heard the woman knock on the door. "It's really really important." She dare not tell Mr. Stone her suspicions in case she was wrong.

Mr. Stone said, "Peter, Chelsea's on the phone. Don't be long."

A second later Peter hesitantly answered.

As quickly as she could, she told him what was happening. "Come right over, will you?"

"I'll be right there."

Chelsea hung up in relief. The woman knocked again, this time more loudly.

Taking a deep breath, Chelsea ran to answer. She opened the door a crack. "Can I help you?"

"Yes, please! Could you do me a big favor?"

Chelsea swallowed hard. "What?"

"I want to talk to Robin, but I don't think she'll talk to me."

Chelsea bit her lip. She had to play for time. "Who?"

"Robin Lockwood."

Chelsea bit back a gasp. Chills ran up and down her spine. "Oh, Robin."

The woman nodded. "I'm Robin's aunt. Her mom and I are twins. When Robin sees me, she might think I'm her momma and run away."

Her aunt! Was it true? "I'm sorry, but I can't let her talk to anyone."

"Are you the baby-sitter?"

"Yes."

"The Osborns should've told you I was coming. I'll stay right out here on the porch with Robin. We'll sit right here on the swing. Please let her come out to see me."

Just then Robin ran up and pushed herself between Chelsea and the door. She saw the woman. "Mom!"

Chelsea frowned. "You said you were her aunt."

"I had to lie." Mrs. Lockwood caught Robin's arm. "I want to talk to you."

"No!" Robin tried to jerk away.

Chelsea caught her free arm and held on. "You can't take her out!"

"Leave her alone!" Jeanna and Bob shouted.

"You're scaring the kids," Chelsea said wildly.

Mrs. Lockwood stopped tugging but still held on to Robin's arm. "I am her mother, and I have every right to talk to her!"

Just then the man walked onto the porch. "What's the holdup?"

Robin saw the man and screamed. "Don't let him beat me again! Let me go! Let me go!" Robin struggled, but her mom wouldn't set her free.

Jeanna and Bob burst into tears.

Suddenly Peter ran onto the porch, his dad right behind him.

"What's going on here?" Mr. Stone asked.

Mrs. Lockwood jumped back from Robin. "It's none of your business."

"They're trying to take Robin!" Chelsea cried, clinging tightly to Robin.

"Call 911," Mr. Stone snapped.

"We're going . . . We're going." Ray Flood caught Mrs. Lockwood's hand and pulled her off the porch. They got back into the gray car and roared away.

"You all right, Chelsea?" Peter asked in concern.

"Yes." Chelsea sighed in relief. She caressed Robin's face. "They're gone. They won't get you."

Robin shivered. "I was scared."

"So were we," Jeanna said, holding Bob's arm.

Mr. Stone clamped a hand on Chelsea's shoulder. "That was quick thinking. I almost didn't let Peter come, but he insisted."

Chelsea smiled at Peter and his dad. "Thanks. I couldn't have handled it alone."

Mr. Stone draped an arm over Peter's shoulder. "You have more strength than I thought, son."

Peter flushed with pleasure.

"I'd better call the Osborns." Chelsea started for the kitchen. "I'll be right back."

"We'll stay until they get back," Mr. Stone said.

Robin smiled up at him. "Want to see my new puppet?"

"All her crafts are great," Jeanna said.

Mr. Stone entered the house, locking the door behind him, and walked away with the kids. Peter hurried to the kitchen with Chelsea.

A few minutes later she reached Mr. Osborn, and he said they'd be right home. Chelsea hung up and sagged against the counter. She looked at Peter with gratitude. "I'm sure glad you came."

"You're brave."

She shrugged.

"I almost went off to play ball instead of coming here."

"I'm glad you didn't!"

"Me too." Peter leaned his elbows on the

counter and hunched his shoulders. "Dad was really surprised when I refused to go with him. I said I had to come here first." He shook his head. "It felt strange having Dad listen to me and do what I wanted instead of what he wanted."

"Why don't you do the same with your photography?"

"I don't have the nerve."

Mr. Stone stepped into the kitchen. "Why not, Peter?"

Chelsea jumped.

Peter's face turned white, and he couldn't speak.

Mr. Stone clamped a hand on Peter's shoulder. "Speak up, son. You did it a while ago. Do it again."

"Tell him," Chelsea whispered.

Peter took a deep breath and squared his shoulders. "Dad, I want to be a photojournalist. I'm good at it, and I'll study hard to be a success at it."

"Well, I'll be." Mr. Stone shook his head, then smiled. "I didn't think you had any plans or goals for the future. I'm impressed."

"Then I can do it?"

"Of course!"

Peter stared at his dad, then laughed and shook his head. "I can't believe it. I thought you'd be mad."

Chelsea heard the Osborns drive in, and she hurried to the door to open it for them.

Later, while the others were in the living room, Peter took Chelsea to the kitchen. "I owe you another one."

Chelsea shook her head.

"I do." He didn't speak for a while. He stared down at his sneakers. "Treva and Joan are cousins."

Chelsea gasped. Had she heard right? "Cousins?"

At last Peter lifted his head. "Their moms are sisters. Treva doesn't want anyone to know because she's really embarrassed at Joan's family being so poor and all."

Chelsea absently pushed her hair back. "Why are you telling me?"

Peter shrugged. "I figured you should know why Treva didn't want you hanging out with Joan."

"Oh! It sort of makes sense now." Chelsea shook her head in wonder. "Is that why you called me Friday night?"

Peter flushed and shook his head. "Treva wanted me to tell you lies about Joan. She already has the whole school convinced Joan is rotten."

"That's awful!"

"Then she called Joan and said she was you."

"No!"

Peter nodded. "Pretending to be you, Treva told Joan she wouldn't teach her photography and wouldn't speak to her ever again."

"So that's why Joan was acting so strange!"

Peter hung his head.

Chelsea doubled her fists. "What else did Treva do that I should know about?"

Peter glanced toward the door. "She called Robin once when you first started coming here. She told Robin she was you and that you weren't coming again."

Chelsea's eyes snapped with anger. "What's her problem anyway?"

"She's jealous of you and your photographs."

"Jealous? She could learn to take good pictures if she tried!"

"That's what I told her, but she wouldn't listen."

Chelsea jabbed Peter's chest. "It's time for you to find a new friend, don't you think?"

He nodded.

Sighing, Chelsea dropped onto a chair and locked her hands on the table. "Now that I know all this stuff, what'll I do?"

"Good question. Get even?"

"I'd like to." Chelsea chuckled dryly. "But I can't. I'm a Christian, and Jesus doesn't want me to get even or to stay angry at Treva."

"You're something else."

Chelsea glanced at the phone. "Maybe I should call Joan right now. But she might not talk to me."

She locked her hands in her lap. "But I have to try. I'll call her when I get home."

But would she have the courage?

The Truth

Chelsea sat at her desk with the Best Friends behind her. She'd told them everything that had happened and what Peter had said. Trembling, she reached for the phone to call Joan. "What if she still won't talk to me?"

Hannah patted Chelsea's shoulder. "Then we'll go see her and make her listen."

"We'll break her door down if we have to." Kathy grinned. "We might even have to push Hank aside."

Frowning, Roxie looked around the room. "Chel, where are all your crafts?"

"Mom packed them away."

"I thought she was going to let you do that, so you'd know what was in what box," Kathy said.

Chelsea's blood ran cold. What if Mom hadn't packed the crafts away? What if something else had happened? Chelsea touched the two red buttons

Joan had left. "What if . . . if Joan stole them to get even?"

Hannah headed for the door. "Where's your mom?"

Chelsea leaped up. "Downstairs. Let's go!" She rushed past Hannah and led the way downstairs. Chelsea's nerves tingled. She found Mom in the kitchen having a peanut butter and jelly sandwich with Dad. The smell of peanut butter was strong.

"Is it a herd of elephants I hear?" Dad asked with a laugh.

Chelsea caught Mom's hand. "Did you pack away my crafts?"

Mom frowned. "Of course not. I knew you'd have to do it, so you'd know what's where."

Chelsea's heart sank.

Dad tugged Chelsea's hair. "Why?"

"They're gone! All of them." Chelsea remembered Robin's doll. "Even Robin's boy doll!"

Mom shook her head. "That's impossible!"

"Joan was here," Hannah said softly.

"But how could she take all the crafts?" Mom's eyes widened. "I remember now! She was upstairs a long time—so long that I thought she'd left without saying good-bye. But how could she carry them away? You have a lot of things."

"Had," Roxie said hoarsely.

Dad pushed himself up. "Let's go have a talk with Joan Golnek."

"Try calling her first," Mom said.

Chelsea ran to the kitchen phone and quickly punched the numbers. Joan answered.

"What did you do with my crafts?"

Joan gasped. "I burned them!" she yelled, then slammed down the receiver.

Chelsea sagged against the counter and burst into tears. "She burned them!"

Dad pulled Chelsea close. "Dry those tears, Chel. We're going to visit that little girl right now! I can't believe she burned them." He turned to the Best Friends. "This is something we'll have to do alone. Chelsea will call you the minute she gets back."

"We'll wait at my house," Roxie said. "Come on, girls."

They said good-bye to Chelsea and slowly walked out.

Mom ran to the stairs and shouted, "Rob, we have to go out a while with Chelsea. Watch Mike."

"Okay, Mom."

Chelsea walked in a daze to the car and slipped onto the backseat. Her head buzzed as Dad drove out of The Ravines. In her mind she saw the pile of crafts blazing high. She could almost hear Sammy crying out. Chelsea moaned and covered her eyes.

Mom reached back and patted Chelsea's leg. "God is always with you, honey."

She nodded and sniffed.

Dad parked at the Golneks', and they all rushed up to the door. Dad knocked.

Mom slipped her arm around Chelsea. "Be strong, hon."

Hank opened the door, saw the McCreas, and tried to slam it shut.

Glenn blocked it with his hand. "Is your dad home?"

"No."

Mom looked around Glenn. "We came to talk to Joan."

"I don't want to talk!" Joan shouted.

Glenn looked at Hank. "Let us in, son. It's better to get this settled."

Hank sighed and nodded. He stepped aside and let them in, then called to Joan. "You might as well as sit down and talk to 'em."

Joan wanted to run away, but she folded her arms and dropped down in Dad's chair. She peeked through her lashes as the McCreas sat on the sofa—a mom and dad and daughter. She only had a brother and a dad. And Dad was never there because he worked too much. Hank perched on the arm of her chair.

"We want the truth, Joan," Billie said softly. "We know you didn't burn Chelsea's crafts. Where are they?"

Joan pressed her lips tightly together. Her mom

never would've gone with her to set things straight. McCrea was really lucky.

Chelsea took a deep breath. "Treva has been making more trouble for both of us."

Her eyes wide, Joan lifted her head. "So?"

"She lied to you." Chelsea told Joan what Peter had said. "I plan to teach you photography. And I plan to get acquainted with you."

Joan sat in stunned silence. She knew Treva hated her, but she hadn't realized how much. Finally she whispered, "I hid your crafts under your brothers' beds."

Chelsea stared at Joan, then burst out laughing.

Joan trembled. She'd expected Chelsea to be angry, but she was laughing. Actually laughing! "The boy doll that was on your desk is on your top closet shelf behind some other things."

"Thank you." Chelsea jumped up. "Want to go home with me, Joan, and look at the crafts?"

"You're welcome to," Mom said, smiling.

Joan darted a look at Hank to see what he thought. He nodded. She turned back to Chelsea. "Sure, I'll go."

"I can start helping you with photography next Monday if you can do it."

"That'll be great." Joan smiled. Was this a dream? It was too good to be true!

Later at home Chelsea set the crafts back in two

neat piles. "I'm glad I don't have to cancel the show. Robin would feel terrible too."

Joan held the boy doll up and laughed. "This is great."

"Robin made it."

"No kidding? Can you show me how?"

Chelsea stared in surprise. "Are you serious?"

Joan nodded. "Don't you think I can learn?"

"Sure, you can. You can learn anything you want to learn."

Joan thought about that for a while, then laughed. "You're right, Chelsea."

Chelsea sucked in her breath. "You called me Chelsea!"

Joan flushed. "It's your name, right?"

"It sure is."

The Best Friends burst through the door. "We couldn't wait a second longer!"

Her face white, Joan backed up against the closet door. Were the girls going to convince Chelsea to kick her out? Maybe they'd even sock her right in the nose.

Chelsea waved her hand at her crafts. "Look, girls! Joan didn't burn them! She hid them . . . in Rob's and Mike's rooms." Chelsea giggled, and the Best Friends joined in.

Later Hannah, Joan, and Kathy lay across Chelsea's bed, and the others sat cross-legged on the floor. They talked about what had happened.

Joan took a deep breath. "I'm sorry for being mean to all of you."

"That's okay," Roxie said gently.

"We understand," Hannah added.

Kathy nudged Joan. "I have a great idea!"

"What?" everyone said at once, then giggled.

"We'll all start a campaign to clear your name at school. Before long the kids will believe us instead of Treva."

Hannah cleared her throat. "Except maybe the girl you socked in the nose in P.E."

Joan flushed. "She was telling lies about Chelsea."

Chelsea helplessly shook her head. "I sure hope you don't do that again."

"I won't." Joan giggled. "Unless somebody lies about you again."

Laughing, Chelsea shook her head again. "Joan, Jesus wants us to *love* others."

"I didn't know that," Joan whispered.

"We'll tell you all about it." Hannah flipped back her black hair and told Joan about Jesus. The others helped.

With tears in her eyes, Chelsea hugged her knees. They'd prayed for Joan, and God had answered!

12

The Big Day

Chelsea jerked the sheet over her head and huddled down into her soft pillow. Oh, she couldn't get up today! How dare she take the things she'd made to the Arts and Crafts Show! How very, very foolish she'd been to think that she was good enough for that.

Butterflies fluttered in her stomach, and little prickles of fear stung her skin. How could she and Robin compete with the others who would be there? Her work was nothing but tacky little homemade things, just like Treva had said. Who would want to buy them? Who would buy a mouse made from an English walnut shell? Or a ladybug made from half a styrofoam ball?

Chelsea moaned. Music drifted in from Mike's room. Smells of freshly brewed coffee and toast slipped under her door and made her stomach churn. Why had she allowed Peter and Robin to talk her into entering the show? If Peter were here right now, she'd make stuffing out of him! She had been crazy to think she could so something like this—or that Robin could either.

Chelsea flipped over and wrapped her arms around her tangled red hair. She'd call Robin and tell her they weren't going. Probably Robin was feeling the same way and would be glad for a way out.

Slowly Chelsea slipped out of her bed. Her Oklahoma T-shirt hung almost to her knees. The carpet felt soft under her bare feet. In her nervousness her phone looked as large as her dresser. It would be easy to call Robin and tell her they weren't going.

Just then someone knocked on her door. She sighed heavily. How could she get her family to understand her decision? "Come in," she said weakly.

The Best Friends swarmed into the room, all talking at once. The smell of chilly air clung to them.

Hooking her hair over her ears, Chelsea stared at them. "What are you doing here so early?"

Hannah circled Chelsea's waist with her arm and grinned. "We voted yesterday to come here this morning."

Roxie tapped Chelsea's arm. "We knew how you'd be feeling."

Kathy nodded. "And we wanted to make sure you didn't decide to stay home."

"You *are* going to the Arts and Crafts Show," they all said at once.

Giggling, Chelsea helplessly shook her head. "I was just about to call Robin and tell her it's off."

"Then we came just in time!" Hannah flung open Chelsea's closet. There were enough clothes there for five girls. "What are you going to wear?"

"My best jeans, the yellow and white blouse, and my yellow sweater."

"We figured you'd decided on your clothes last night." Kathy opened the bottom dresser drawer and pulled out the soft yellow sweater. "Very excellent choice."

Roxie found Chelsea's jeans and blouse while Hannah made the bed.

Chelsea smiled weakly at the Best Friends. "Can I really do it?"

"Yes!"

Chelsea took a deep breath and slowly let it out. "All right!" She grinned. "Thanks for coming. I'm okay now. I won't back out."

"Good!"

"We'll help load the station wagon while you take a shower." Hannah picked up a box of crafts. "See you downstairs in a few minutes."

Grinning, Roxie shook her finger at Chelsea. "If you take too long, we'll drag you down." Roxie picked up another box and followed Hannah.

"You're a success!" Kathy squeezed Chelsea's

hand, then picked up a box and hurried after Roxie and Hannah.

Chelsea laughed as she walked to the bathroom. She heard the Best Friends coming back up for another load. What would she do without them? She couldn't imagine.

"Thank You for my best friends, Heavenly Father," Chelsea whispered.

Several minutes later she ran lightly downstairs to the kitchen. Mom already had breakfast ready for her. Chelsea kissed Mom's cheeks. "Thanks."

"I want you to have plenty of energy for this wonderful day."

Suddenly hungry, Chelsea sat at the table. She drank the small glass of orange juice. She ate an egg, a piece of bacon, and a slice of whole wheat toast. Just as she finished, Dad walked in, brushing his hands together.

"Your friends helped me load the wagon. They said they'd see you at the show." Dad kissed the top of Chelsea's head. "I'm ready when you are."

Chelsea hugged him. He smelled of soap and aftershave. "I love you, Daddy!"

"I love you." He tugged her hair and rubbed a hand over the arm of her soft sweater. "You look beautiful, as usual."

She flushed.

Mom held Chelsea close. "We know how much

courage it's taking you to go today. We're proud of you, honey."

Chelsea's eyes filled with tears. "Thanks."

A few minutes later Chelsea walked with Dad into the community center that was set up with dozens of tables for the arts and crafts. She carried the tablecloth, and Dad carried in the first box. Men and women scurried about, filling their tables with their products. Voices echoed in the large room. Chelsea bit her lip. Was she really ready for all this? She'd already received her table number, so she hurried to the empty ten-foot table. She spread the blue cloth over it and pinned her sign in place while Dad hurried out for more things.

She glanced to the table at her left. A man with a nose like a moose was setting candle holders and other tin items in place. He smiled at Chelsea, and she smiled back. To her right a woman with all kinds of things made of wood was hanging her sign— WOOD WORKS BY CARLA. Chelsea glanced at her sign. It was a beautiful sign Mom had painted— CRAFTS BY CHELSEA AND ROBIN.

Chelsea turned and almost bumped into Robin. The little girl's face was so pale, her freckles disappeared.

"I'm real scared," Robin whispered as she nervously tugged her green sweater down over her jeans.

Chelsea pulled Robin close. "We're here together, and God is here with us."

Robin stepped back and wiped her eyes. She took a deep breath. "Mr. and Mrs. Osborn are bringing in my things. They prayed with me again this morning. They said to tell you they know we'll do good today."

"My mom and dad said we would too."

Robin leaned close to Chelsea. "Last night I dreamed nobody bought anything."

Chelsea smiled reassuringly. "It was only a dream."

"Are you sure?"

Chelsea nodded. "We'll sell our things! Just wait and see!"

13

The First Sale

Later Chelsea stood alone at the table while Robin ran to help Gwen Osborn carry in another box. Sounds of laughter and talking rang back and forth across the room and bounced up to the steel beam rafters.

Mel Osborn set a box on the floor beside the table, tugged his jacket in place, and turned to Chelsea. "Gwen and I want to thank you again for what you did for Robin."

Chelsea squirmed uncomfortably. She didn't need or want more thanks. "I'm glad I could help."

"She's a new girl since she opened up to you. She still doesn't trust us totally, but she's learning—especially after last Sunday."

"What happened to Mrs. Lockwood and Ray Flood?"

"Nobody knows. They probably left the state so Flood wouldn't be arrested."

"I'm sure Robin feels better."

Mel nodded. "I hadn't realized how frightened of Flood she was. But now she knows we'll always be around to keep her safe."

"That's good."

"And she wants to learn about Jesus! I guess that's the best news."

"It sure is! I like Robin. It's been fun doing crafts with her. She has a lot of talent."

"I know. I'm going to see that she has materials on hand to keep creating things." Mel smiled at Chelsea. "I'd better finish unloading before the crowd comes. Thanks again, Chelsea."

Smiling, Chelsea watched him walk away. The day was suddenly brighter. With a soft laugh she turned back to the display case Dad had set up. She carefully arranged a shelf of rag dolls of various sizes. She picked up a small pink gingham doll with big blue eyes and pink yarn hair. She held the doll close. Could she part with her? Chelsea sighed and slowly set the doll in place.

"Chelsea McCrea?"

She turned to find Treva Joerger's mother standing there with a clipboard in her hands. A ring sparkled from almost every finger. Wearing a red skirt and jacket with a white blouse, she looked more like Treva's sister than her mother. "Hi, Mrs. Joerger."

She gazed at the table, then looked at Chelsea in admiration. "You have a beautiful display!"

Chelsea could barely find her voice. "Thank you."

"I wish more young people would join the show." Mrs. Joerger sounded sad, but then she smiled at Chelsea. "I wish you the best of luck today."

Chelsea bit back a surprised gasp. "Thank you." She'd thought Mrs. Joerger would act like Treva.

"People will start coming soon. Officially we aren't open until 10, but folks like to come early to look at everything." Mrs. Joerger jotted something on the paper attached to her clipboard. "We'll stay until 9 tonight. You'll be in charge of your own area, so please make sure it's clean and that nothing is left behind."

Chelsea nodded.

With a soft laugh Mrs. Joerger picked up a ladybug on a leaf. "I like this. I think I'll buy it for myself."

Chelsea shook her head in astonishment. "Oh no, Mrs. Joerger! You can't buy it!"

Mrs. Joerger lifted her fine brows. "Oh?"

"I'd like to give it to you. I wouldn't feel right to make you buy it." Chelsea nervously rubbed her hands down her jeans.

Mrs. Joerger laughed and shook her head. "My

dear, I wouldn't feel right just taking it. Here's the money. And the price is more than fair."

Chelsea shook her head.

"Now, don't hesitate to take it. You'll be doing this all day long. People will be very glad to pay for these delightful crafts. Not everyone is gifted enough to be able to create original crafts like these." Smiling, Mrs. Joerger shook her finger at Chelsea. "You're doing them a favor by allowing them to buy your work."

Reluctantly Chelsea dropped the money into the appropriate compartment of her money box. Finally she smiled. "Thanks for wanting the ladybug, and thank you very much for the nice words. I was afraid my things weren't good enough."

"You needn't feel that way at all. I've been doing this for a long time, and I think your display compares favorably with any I've seen." Mrs. Joerger brushed a strand of blonde hair off her cheek. "I'll be back later to see how you're doing." She smiled and walked to the next table to talk to the man with the big nose.

Robin rushed up, her face flushed and glowing. "Did she really buy something?"

"Yes."

Robin clapped and spun around. "Our first sale! And it's not even time to open!" She took a deep breath and finally calmed down enough to arrange four of her puppets. She held one against herself with her eyes closed.

Chelsea smiled. She knew what Robin was thinking and feeling. It's hard to part with something you've made with your own hands.

Glenn McCrea stopped at the table with the last box. He hugged Chelsea and winked at Robin. "Let me know if you girls need anything. Mike and Rob will be around later. And so will your mom, Chel." He turned to go, then turned back. "Keep up your courage and you'll do just fine. God is with you."

"Thanks, Dad." Chelsea watched him walk away. She wanted to call him back, but she didn't.

Robin held up several dollars. "I'm going to look at the other things before it's time to open. But I'll be back on time to help you sell." She grinned. "I don't think I'll find anything I'll want more than this." She touched her favorite puppet.

Chelsea chuckled as Robin hurried away. Chelsea set a few more things on the table, then stood back to look at it. It did look good!

At a sound behind her she whirled around. Treva stood there, scowling with anger.

"I didn't think you'd really have the nerve to come with your stuff!" Treva angrily waved her hand in an arc to take in the table. "They'll never sell. Who would pay good money for tacky little homemade things?"

Chelsea laughed. "Your mother."

Treva's eyes widened. "My mother?"

"She paid good money for a ladybug I made."

Treva jerked back. "You're making that up!"

Chelsea shrugged. "Ask her."

"I certainly will!"

"She said I'll sell my work because it's good. She should know. It is her business to know." Chelsea took a step toward Treva. "Is there anything else you want to bring up?" Chelsea wanted to say, "Like maybe your cousin Joan," but she didn't.

Treva flipped back her long blonde hair. "It's too bad Peter even told you about the show."

"It was your idea."

Treva scowled. "Don't remind me."

Chelsea laughed and stepped even closer to Treva. "I'll thank him when I see him."

Treva whirled around and stormed off.

With a concerned look on his face, John Alexander came to stand at Chelsea's side. "Are you all right?"

Chelsea nodded. "Treva can't hurt me anymore."

"Good." John rested his hands lightly on his lean hips and glanced around. "Where's Robin?"

"Looking at the displays. She'll be back soon."

John narrowed his eyes. "How's she doing?"

"Great!"

"I'm glad. I apologized to the Osborns for yelling at Robin. They were really nice about it."

Just then Robin ran to the table. She smiled at John, and he smiled back.

Chelsea watched them together, thankful Robin held no hard feelings for John.

He picked up a cross-stitch picture of a robin. "My sister would like this." He reached into his pocket and pulled out some money.

Chelsea shook her head. "You take it as my gift, John. Please."

He smiled. "Thanks. But don't give your things away to others."

"I won't," Chelsea said.

"You two have a wonderful day." Smiling, John lifted his hand and walked away.

Robin nudged Chelsea and whispered, "Here comes a big crowd of people."

Chelsea's heart leaped. She turned and watched the mass of people flow through the open doors. "Let's get behind the table where we belong, Robin."

"I'm sooo excited!"

They stepped into place as several people stopped at the table to look at their display. No one laughed at the crafts or called them tacky little homemade things.

"You do beautiful work," a short, plump woman wearing a flowered dress said as she held up a yellow gingham doll with yellow yarn hair. "I want this for my little granddaughter. She'll love it."

Chelsea took the money and dropped it into the cash box as Robin talked to a girl about a puppet.

Chelsea glanced around at the laughing, talking crowd. The Arts and Crafts Show had begun! Stepping close to Robin, Chelsea pressed her hand to her heart and smiled.

14

A Long Exciting Day

Chelsea tipped up the can of soda and drank thankfully. The cold sting of the carbonated water and the sweet taste of orange refreshed her. Her feet ached, and she was tired, but she couldn't quit yet. There were three hours left. Smells of popcorn and hot dogs wafted around the room. She smiled at Robin, who sat cross-legged on a crate eating a sandwich and drinking orange juice from a paper cup. "You really should go home, Robin."

"No way! I want to stay until the end. I'm not a bit tired."

"If you do get too tired, tell me. You've worked really hard today. I couldn't have done it without you."

"It's the most fun I ever had!" Robin's eyes sparkled, and she looked different than the sullen girl of two weeks ago.

"It has been great, hasn't it?" Chelsea set the

empty soda can on the floor under the table. "Next year we'll have even more things."

Laughing, Robin nodded. "We might even need *two* tables!"

"We probably will."

Chelsea saw the Best Friends in the crowd. They'd stopped earlier with an offer to stay at the table so Chelsea could look around. She'd taken them up on her offer, but had hurried back because the table was her responsibility.

A woman with dark hair stepped up to the table. "I'd like three puppets just alike if you have them."

Chelsea turned to Robin. "Check the box under the table—the box nearest to you."

Robin did and pulled out three puppets. "Are these all right?"

"They're perfect!" The woman paid for them and left.

Another woman held up a styrofoam mouse glued to a mouse trap. "How much is this, dear?"

Chelsea knew the tag was clearly marked, but she patiently quoted the price. The woman walked away without buying the mouse. That didn't bother Chelsea at all. The first time it had happened she'd almost cried. Now she was used to it.

A short man with a beard bought two stuffed animals. "I wish my daughter would've come."

"Does she make crafts?" Chelsea asked as she put the animals in a bag.

"No. Oil paintings. And she's good! But she's afraid others won't think so."

Chelsea nodded. "That's how I felt at first, but I was wrong. Tell her to talk to me about it." Chelsea jotted down her name and phone number on the paper bag that held the animals and gave it to the man. "I'll tell her how much fun it is. That might give her the courage to come next year since I've been here and know how great it is."

"You're right. Thanks." He smiled, then walked away.

"The table sure looks empty," Robin whispered.

Just then Mrs. Joerger stopped at the table. She looked as neat and cheerful as she had early that morning. "You've sold a lot of things! How wonderful. I've heard good comments about your table. I'm pleased, and I'm sure you are too."

"We are," Chelsea and Robin said at the same time. They looked at each other and chuckled.

Mrs. Joerger stayed a little longer, then walked to the next table. The man with the nose like a moose had also sold a lot of things.

A dark-haired boy who could barely see over the table said, "I have 89 cents, and I want to buy something. What can I get?"

Chelsea glanced over the table, then picked up

the tiny cottonball kitten. It was marked $1.00, but she offered it to the boy for 89 cents.

He touched it and laughed. "I like it." He handed Chelsea the money, then rubbed the kitten against his cheek as he walked away.

Just then Joan Golnek walked up. "That was nice of you, McCrea."

"Chelsea, you mean."

Joan flushed and nodded.

Chelsea chuckled. "It'll get easier as you say it." She pulled Robin to her side. "Joan, this is Robin, my partner. Robin, Joan wants to learn how to make crafts and do photography too."

Robin frowned. "Are you the girl who was so mean to Chelsea?"

Joan's stomach tightened, and she nodded.

"But no longer," Chelsea said quickly. "Now we're friends."

Friends! Joan hugged the word to her. She'd never had a friend before.

Before they could talk more, several people stopped at the table, keeping Chelsea and Robin busy.

Joan walked slowly away. She looked across the room and spotted Hannah, Kathy, and Roxie. They looked her way at the same time and motioned for her to join them. She hesitated. Were they really asking her to come, or was it someone behind her? She glanced back, but no one else was looking toward the girls. Joan's heart leaped, and she hurried over to the girls. Before she reached them someone caught her arm.

"Joan! It is you!"

Her heart sank. It was Treva's mom. "Hi, Aunt Mavis."

"You're looking well."

"So are you." Joan wanted to run away as fast as she could. Mom once had looked like Aunt Mavis, but no longer. Before she'd left home, she'd not only stopped taking care of the family but of herself too.

"Treva said you ran off to be with your mom."

Frowning, Joan shook her head. She'd never do that. "We don't even know where she is!"

Mrs. Joerger bit her lip and looked sad. "I just don't understand Shirley, even though she is my sister. She has a fine husband and two good kids."

Joan moved restlessly.

"If you ever need anything, let me know." Mrs. Joerger squeezed Joan's hand. "I wish you would've let me pay your way into the Photography Club. I sent the money with Treva, but she brought it back and said you weren't interested."

Anger rushed through Joan. "Treva was wrong! I did want to join, and I still do!"

"I wonder why Treva didn't know."

Joan opened her mouth to tell the truth about

Treva, then decided not to. Getting even just wasn't important to her anymore.

Mrs. Joerger shrugged. "I don't have my purse right now, but I'll see you get the money to join the club."

"Thanks anyway, Aunt Mavis. I'll get my own money."

"How?"

Joan smiled. "Doing odd jobs. I know a bunch of kids called *King's Kids* who do odd jobs as a business. I'm going to join them to make enough money for the Photography Club."

"Good for you, Joan! I'm proud of you." Mrs. Joerger briefly hugged Joan. "Please come visit, will you? I miss you. And your mom. She and I had a lot of fun together when we were children. I really miss her."

Joan didn't say anything.

They talked a minute longer. Then Mrs. Joerger hurried away, and Joan rushed over to the girls. She told them about her conversation with her aunt, and they comforted her. She wanted to hug every one of them and tell them they were wonderful, but she was too shy. Maybe someday she'd be able to tell them how much they'd helped her.

At their crafts table Chelsea breathed a sigh of relief when the last customer walked away. It seemed like she and Robin were either standing and waiting or were being swamped by people—there was nothing in between.

Robin opened her cash box. "I'm going to count my money again. I can't believe how much I've made so far." She'd counted it about ten times already.

Chelsea glanced in her cash box. She'd made a whole lot more than she'd dreamed possible. She heard someone stop, and she glanced up to see Peter and Treva standing there. Her heart dropped to her feet.

"Hi, Chelsea." Peter smiled.

Treva jabbed him in the ribs with her elbow. "Don't even try to be nice to her!" Treva slammed a bag on the table. "I want my money back now!"

Chelsea frowned. "You didn't buy anything."

"My mom did, and she says she doesn't want it." Treva pulled out the ladybug on a leaf. "Look at it! It's ugly! So give back the money right now."

Chelsea's mind whirled, but then she understood. "I don't believe you, Treva," Chelsea said coldly. "Your mom wants that ladybug."

"She changed her mind. Right, Peter?"

Chelsea studied Peter intently. His face was red, and he looked as if he wanted to leave. "Well, Peter? Is Treva telling the truth?"

Just then the Best Friends and Joan stopped behind Peter and Treva, but they didn't say anything.

Treva jabbed Peter again. "Don't just stand there like a dummy! Tell her!"

"Tell me," Chelsea said softly. "This is a good time to start telling the truth about Treva."

Peter cleared his throat. "Mrs. Joerger doesn't know Treva brought it back."

"What?" Treva shrieked, looking at Peter in anger and shock.

"Thanks." Chelsea pushed the bag into Treva's hands. "Give it back to your mom."

Her face red, Treva turned on Peter. "Just see if I ever do a favor for you again!"

"You won't need to." Peter squared his shoulders. "I'll be too busy to hang out with you ever again."

"You don't mean that!"

Peter nodded. "I sure do."

Chelsea laughed under her breath. She enjoyed watching Peter break free of Treva, and she knew Joan and the Best Friends did too.

Peter tapped the bag in Treva's hand. "You're going to have to return that yourself. I won't help you sneak it into the back room where you found it. Maybe you'll get caught—and then maybe your mom can help you learn right from wrong so you don't grow up to be a cheat like you are now."

Treva's eyes flashed, and she stamped her foot. "You're the cheat, and I'll make sure *everybody* knows it."

Joan tapped Treva on the shoulder. "Knows what, *cousin*?"

Treva gulped and turned bright red. "What are you doing here?"

"She's with us," the Best Friends said, grinning.

Treva's eyes almost popped out of her head.

"We know she's your cousin," Chelsea said. "And we know you've been spreading stories about her around school. You must stop doing that." Chelsea stabbed a finger at Treva. "And you will not spread bad stories about Peter either!"

"We all know what you are," Hannah said sternly. "And we won't let you hurt anyone else."

"That's right." Peter nodded. "I'll help these girls make sure you don't hurt anybody else." He pushed his face close to Treva. "And I know plenty to tell about you if you ever spread another story!"

Treva's eyes filled with tears. Sobbing, she ran away, the bag clutched to her chest.

Chelsea let out her breath and leaned weakly against the table. "I hate to fight with anyone, but I know we had to stop Treva—for her own sake and for ours."

Joan nodded. "Who knows—maybe someday we can be friends with her."

"Highly unlikely," Peter said.

Chelsea and the Best Friends looked at each other and smiled. They knew God worked miracles.

All they had to do was look at Robin and Joan and even Peter to prove that.

Several customers stopped at the table, so Peter, Joan, and the Best Friends drifted away, talking a mile a minute.

Chelsea felt a pang of regret that she couldn't go with them, then shook her head. She was happy right where she was. She knew they'd be back later to help load the few things that were left. Best friends always helped each other.

A woman held up a mouse and frowned at Chelsea. "Did you really make this?"

"No."

"I thought not!"

Holding in a chuckle, Chelsea motioned to Robin. "*She* did."

The woman gasped in surprise. "How can that be? It's a fine piece of work! I've never seen anything like it."

"That's because it's one of a kind," Robin said proudly. "I designed it and made it myself."

The woman stroked the mouse. "I'll buy it! How much is it?"

Chelsea knew the tag was in plain sight, but Robin patiently told her the price. The lady paid for it and walked to the next table.

Chelsea hugged Robin. "We had a great day, didn't we?"

"The best!" Robin picked up her favorite puppet. "I'm glad this didn't sell."

Chelsea laughed and whispered, "Why don't you put it in a box before it does."

Robin giggled. "That's a great idea!" She bent down to the box and dropped the puppet inside and pulled out the boy doll. "I saved this too."

"You did?"

Robin held it out to Chelsea. "It's yours. I want you to have it as a gift from me."

Tears pricked Chelsea's eyes as she slowly took the boy doll. "Thank you. I'll keep it forever!"

Just then a woman stopped at the table and pointed to the boy doll. "I'll take that."

Chelsea held it to her. "I'm sorry. It's not for sale."

Robin slipped a puppet on her hand and waved it around. "How about this instead? It's real cute."

The woman frowned and finally nodded. "How much is it?"

Robin told her and took her money. "I'll have boy dolls next year if you want to come back then."

The woman smiled. "I'll keep that in mind." She walked away just as the Best Friends and Joan returned.

"Your dad said it's time to close up and take your things to the car," Hannah said.

Chelsea giggled. "Mostly we have empty boxes." She had five puppets left. She put each into a bag, then held them out to her friends. "These are my gifts to you. You can take them with you when you baby-sit."

Joan drew back. Was Chelsea really giving her a gift?

"Here, Joan." Chelsea pushed a bag into Joan's hand. "As a *King's Kid* you'll get a lot of baby-sitting jobs."

"Thanks, Chelsea," Joan whispered. Her heart was almost bursting with joy.

The Best Friends pulled theirs out and started a puppet show on the spot.

Giggling, Robin leaned against Chelsea and watched.

Joan pulled her puppet out of the bag, slipped it on her hand, and joined in with the show.

Chelsea smiled proudly. She had the very best friends in the whole entire world!

Robin pushed her favorite puppet onto Chelsea's hand. "Use mine."

"Thanks." Chelsea slipped it on and joined the show.

You are invited to become a *Best Friends Member!*

In becoming a member you'll receive a club membership card with your name on the front and a list of the Best Friends and their favorite Bible verses on the back along with a space for your favorite Scripture. You'll also receive a colorful, 2-inch, specially-made I'M A BEST FRIEND button and a write-up about the author, Hilda Stahl, with her autograph. As a bonus you'll get an occasional newsletter about the upcoming BEST FRIENDS books.

All you need to do is mail your NAME, ADDRESS (printed neatly, please), AGE and $3.00 for postage and handling to:

BEST FRIENDS
P.O. Box 96
Freeport, MI 49325

WELCOME TO THE CLUB!

(Authorized by the author, Hilda Stahl)